I0689303

Also by Paul Betit

Phu Bai
Kagnew Station
The Man In The Canal

Let Me Tell A Story

A Mix of Short Fiction and Memoir

Paul Betit

Copyright 2016 Paul Betit

All rights reserved. No part of this publication may be reproduced (except
for reviews), stored in a retrieval system, or transmitted in any form by any
means, electronic, mechanical, photocopying, recording or otherwise, without the
prior written permission of the publisher and author.

ISBN-13: 9780990897163
ISBN-10: 0990897168

Library of Congress Control Number: 2016913026
BeeMan Books, Brunswick, ME

Published by BeeMan Books
Box 384
Brunswick, Maine 04011

Printed in the United States of America

A FEW WORDS FROM THE AUTHOR

Let Me Tell A Story is quite a departure from the military crime novels I have published in the past. Written in the same tight but detailed style characteristic of my earlier books, these stories are a mix of fiction and memoir. Each of these tales was inspired by actual events.

Although written in the first person, the narrator of one story is not necessarily the narrator of another story.

A lot of these stories were influenced by my Vietnam experience — how it affected me then and to this day.

The stories, some of which are set in Maine, are arranged in chronological order over a sixty-year period.

It starts with a tale about a boy who learns some life lessons during a trip with his family to Maine's northern-most Aroostook County. It ends with a short tale about a husband and wife who are learning lessons of their own while trying to come to grips with old age. In between are stories about young soldiers and old soldiers, husbands and wives, fathers and mothers and other sordid types.

Paul Betit
Brunswick, Maine

To my grandson, Alex, who continuously inspires me

Trip
To
Sinclair

August 1959

I was twelve going on thirteen when my family travelled from Augusta to the little village of Sinclair in Maine's northern-most Aroostook County. It was the first time we all spent a night away from home. It was our first real trip as a family.

To prepare, I paid a quarter for a Maine highway map at the Mobil station on the west-side rotary. I used a pencil to trace our route north. I memorized it.

Interstate 95 didn't extend beyond Augusta. Construction of the turnpike had been completed more than three years before, but the toll road didn't go any farther north than the Maine capital. It was two hundred eighty miles from Augusta to the little village of Sinclair in Aroostook County. My father said it would take all day to get there, and it did.

Mama said we were making the trip north so Pepere, her father, could meet his new granddaughter. Belle was six months old. According to my calculations my baby sister brought the total number of grandchildren to twenty; some of whom I had never met or barely knew.

We didn't have a car. We made the trip in my father's 1953 three-quarter-ton Dodge pickup truck. It was the model with the front grill that looked like it was stuck in a permanent frown.

My parents sat up front in the cab with the baby, while my brother Teddy and I were relegated to the truck bed.

The Dodge was not just the family car. Most mornings, it also served as a garbage truck.

My father worked the swing shift as an aide on a mental health ward out at the VA Center in Togus. During the week, he spent his mornings picking up rubbish at private homes, apartment buildings and small businesses in Augusta and Hallowell. He earned enough money from his two jobs to enable my mother to stay home with us kids.

For our trip, my father had removed the black sideboards that had **YOU CALL WE HAUL** and our telephone number emblazoned on them in large white letters.

My brother and I still could tell it was a rubbish truck though. When we sat on the truck bed, we detected a slight odor of decay that just never went away, and, as the truck headed up Route 2, little pieces of grit flew up, stinging our eyes.

"This stinks," Teddy said. My little brother was already a master at stating the obvious.

We tried standing up looking forward over the roof of the cab, but we couldn't hear each other talk. The wind whipped past carrying our words away. We had to shout to be heard.

When we turned and stood with our backs against the cab, we could speak in more normal voices but it wasn't as much fun. It was much better to see where we were going instead of watching where we had been.

We spent much of the trip looking forward, and we didn't talk much.

Normally, I wore a crew cut during the summer. When school was done, the barber would trim my hair nearly down to my scalp. This year though, I let it grow. Mama said it was all right. It had been nearly three months since my last visit to the barber, and my hair had come in dark and wavy. I could feel the wind pass through it as I stood in the back of the truck. I liked that.

The trip was not uneventful.

My mother had packed a picnic lunch. It was stored in a wooden hamper up against the tailgate. Next to it sat my gym bag, which held the highway map, a hardcover copy of *Johnny Tremaine* I had borrowed from the library, two changes of underwear and socks, a t-shirt, a pair of long pants and my bathing trunks. A suitcase containing the rest of the family's clothing sat next to my bag.

Teddy's hula hoop was pinned under the suitcase. The woman who lived across the street from us said my little brother was part Hawaiian. Two years younger than I was, he liked to show off. He *was* really good at making the plastic hoop spin around his waist.

Near Albion, Teddy crept to the rear of the truck and opened the picnic hamper. A half-dozen paper napkins immediately went fluttering over the tailgate. He slammed the lid shut and scrambled back to the front of the truck.

"Don't say a word," Teddy said. "Maybe Mama won't notice."

About two hours after our trip started, we pulled close to Bangor. As we rolled slowly past Dow Air Force Base, I could see machine guns poking out of the canopy of a bomber parked amid the trees surrounding this side of the base.

In Bangor, my father stopped at an Esso station on Main Street to top off the gas. The ten gallons cost two dollars and fifty cents. He didn't have enough money in his wallet, so my mother fished a dollar from her purse to make up the difference.

Still following Route 2, we stopped to eat lunch. Somewhere north of Medway, Papa pulled the truck off the highway onto a short stretch of road that was no longer in use. We sat munching on bologna sandwiches while sitting among the weeds sprouting up between the cracks in the decaying tarmac.

Mama poured milk from a bottle into small paper cups. It was a little warm. She also handed out soggy strips of cucumber. Then she rummaged through the picnic basket.

"I guess I forgot to pack the napkins," Mama observed.

Teddy didn't say a word. Neither did I.

A short time later, as we drove through the woods above Lincoln, Teddy and I began to sing *The Lollipop Song* at the top of our lungs, banging on the roof with our hands to recreate its guitar lick.

Suddenly, Papa pulled the truck off onto the shoulder and popped out of the cab.

"Cut out that crap, or I'll come up there and cut it out for you," he yelled up at us. "You're driving your mother nuts. Stop banging on the friggin' roof."

Before climbing back into the truck's cab, Papa shouted to Mama in French. When he was in, he slammed the door so hard the truck rocked.

"What did he say?" Teddy asked.

"I don't know," I answered. "You know I don't understand one word of French."

We lived in the south end of Augusta across town from Sand Hill, where most of the kids were taught to speak French and English at St. Augustine's School. But French wasn't taught at the school we went to, and we weren't encouraged to speak it at home. Mama and Papa used the language as a secret code. When they wanted to talk about a subject they didn't want my brother and me to know about they spoke French.

We followed Route 2 until it merged with U.S. Route 1 near Caribou, and traveled on this highway for at least another hour.

When we slowed down to drive through New Sweden, where the potato fields had already bloomed, Teddy took another trip toward the rear of the truck bed. This time, he tried to retrieve his hula hoop, but when he slid it out from under the suitcase, the truck rolled over a bump and he lost his grip on the piece of plastic tubing. It bounced out of the back of the truck. Teddy mouthed a drawn-out "shit" as he watched the hoop take a couple of big bounces before rolling down the road away from the truck. "Don't let Mama hear you say that word," I told him. "She'll wash your mouth out with soap. I know."

We passed the final half-hour of the trip in silence, traveling up Route 161 for twenty five miles or so through the woods to Sinclair.

When he retired several years before, my grandfather moved from Augusta to Sinclair with my grandmother, who had since died. Mama said Pepere wanted to return to The County, where he was born, to be near where he spent most of his early life growing potatoes on a farm in the Canadian province of New Brunswick.

A few years after World War I ended my grandfather had moved his family to Maine from New Brunswick, where Mama was born. He spent the next thirty years or so in Augusta working primarily as a carpenter. Now, he lived alone in a little bungalow in a small hamlet on the southwest shore of Long Lake.

I didn't know Pepere well. My mother once told me we lived with her folks for two years after I was born. I didn't remember that.

The only memory I had of my grandfather was from an event that occurred when I was about three years old. He worked on a crew installing a new roof on our house on Child Street, and I climbed up the long extension ladder to see him. I don't know why, but I had a powerful urge to be with him that day. I could still remember the shocked look on his face when he glanced up from the asphalt shingle he was about to nail into place to see me standing next to him on the scaffold.

I probably didn't spend much time up on the roof, but I did get the first spanking I could remember that day. "Don't you ever do that again," my mother told me in between whacks to my behind.

I wasn't allowed out of the house until the roofers were done. I don't recall Pepere ever coming to our home again.

When I asked my mother what my grandfather was like just prior to our trip, she answered: "Oh, you will see." She never told me what anybody was like. If she had opinions about people, she kept them to herself. I guess she wanted me to figure out those things on my own.

We arrived in Sinclair a little after four o'clock. After we parked in the graveled driveway behind a Chrysler sedan and an old Ford pickup, we entered the bungalow through a side door that opened into the kitchen. We trooped through the kitchen to find my grandfather waking up from an afternoon nap on a daybed at one end of the enclosed sun porch that looked out over the lake.

Pepere looked a lot different than the man I had seen when I climbed up the ladder to the roof nearly a decade before. His hair had become whiter. As he stood to greet us I could see he now walked with a pronounced stoop. In my world, where most people were older than me, he was the oldest person I had ever met.

At first, it was difficult to tell whether Pepere was glad to see us. His expression didn't seem to change much. He looked like he had just eaten something sour. My grandfather's voice had become hoarse. That, coupled with his accent, made it difficult for me to understand him at first. I really had to listen.

When he sat down at the kitchen table with my parents, the talk gradually lapsed into French. That left me out of the conversation. After fifteen minutes of trying to decipher what was said, I slipped unnoticed out the door.

I walked out to the end of the driveway and looked up and down the road. Nothing. Then someone called out to me. "Hey, kid. What'd ya doing?"

On the other side of the road stood a boy about two or three years older and nearly a full head taller than me.

"Visiting my Pepere," I called back.

The boy motioned. "Come here," he said. "I'll show you around."

His name was Butch. He lived in a little farm across the road from my grandfather.

I could hear cows lowing as we walked up the driveway to the barn.

A flock of chickens pecked their way across the barnyard; their heads bobbing up and down as they scratched the ground searching for a tasty morsel.

"I don't think most of these birds are long for this world," Butch said. "None of them are laying hardly at all."

We stepped into the small barn, where Butch's dad sat on a stool patiently squeezing milk from the udder of a large black-and-white cow.

Butch made the introductions. "Hi'ya kid," his father said. "Want some milk?" While grasping the top of the cow's teat with his thumb and forefinger, Butch's dad bent the udder slightly, pointed it at me and sent a narrow spray of milk in my direction. He laughed. Then he turned on his stool and concentrated on aiming the liquid into a bucket under the cow.

As we turned to leave, Butch's father called out, "Make sure you clean the milking parlor once I'm done with Blackie."

After stepping back into the barnyard, Butch lamented: "I do all the dirty work. I just finished mucking out the stalls and watering the herd."

The "herd" consisted of six large Holsteins. "We only got six cows and three of them aren't giving milk," Butch said. His family sold milk to some of their neighbors. "Hardly worth doing this any more."

Butch led me back across the road to show me another part of his family's operation. It was a small sawmill, tucked along the shoreline between Pepere's house and another bungalow a little further down the road.

Work was finished for the day. Butch showed me the large circular saw used to rip long lengths of logs into lumber. He pointed out various lengths of neatly-stacked boards and explained the use for each one.

"Tomorrow is Saturday, and the crew will work just a half-day," Butch said. "You can come and watch if you want."

As Butch and I stood talking next to the road, a girl about my age came walking toward us from the direction of the village we had driven through on the way to Pepere's. She wore a light blue, short-sleeved blouse and dark shorts. Her short wavy hair was nearly jet-black. As she walked closer, I could see her eyes were nearly as dark as her hair, and she wore just a hint of pink lipstick. As she passed by, she greeted us with a cheery "*bonjour*" in a soft lilting voice.

"Who is that?" I whispered to Butch. "What did she say?"

"Her name is Yvonne, and she said hello," Butch replied. "She speaks French."

"Oh," I said, watching the girl walk away.

"Look out for her," Butch warned. "She likes boys."

When I went back to the bungalow, I found Pepere sitting down by his wooden dock, scaling a bucket of fish.

"Yellow perch," he said. "Took the putt-putt and caught them this morning on Mud Lake." When my grandfather motioned in the direction of the main village to show me where that lake was located, I noticed the small wooden boat moored to his dock. "Not much in it but perch, horn pout and suckers."

When we had crossed into Sinclair, we had crossed a bridge over a stream about a quarter-mile from Pepere's house. Maybe that narrow channel connected Long Lake with Mud Lake.

Pepere handed me his small scaling knife. He showed me how to hold the fish and work the knife from tail to head, going over the body several times to peel the scales from the fish. Then my grandfather reached into his tackle box and pulled out a knife with a serrated blade.

"When we get back to the kitchen, I'll fillet these fish," he said, while deftly working his knife on a fish. "Your mama will roll them in batter and fry them up. A good supper she will make."

I counted about twenty little fish in the bucket. My grandfather did most of the work. By the time we were done I had managed to remove the scales from just four of them.

"Good work!" my grandfather said as we got up from the dock and began walking back to the house. "Just like old times." He smiled for a moment. "You and me together."

"Huh?" I responded.

"You don't remember?" My grandfather stopped walking. "When you were little, you folks lived with me and Memere for a while."

I didn't remember.

"I would help your mother get you breakfast in the morning," he said, "and you would always be there to greet me when I came home at night after work."

I vainly tried to recall that. Then the light went on.

"I do remember one thing, Pepere," I said excitedly. "I remember climbing up on the roof to see you."

My grandfather walked on.

"Oh yes," he said. "We both got into a lot of trouble for that one."

I recalled only the trouble I was in. I never knew my grandfather got into trouble, too. Maybe that was why he didn't visit us.

The breaded perch turned out to be a good supper, just as Pepere said it would.

That night, I slept out on the porch on the day bed, while Teddy, who was a bed wetter, spent the night alone in the truck sleeping on a rubber mat. "You better not piss on the seat," Papa warned my brother as he climbed into the cab.

Belle slept between my parents on an old Castro convertible in the living room in the part of the house facing the road.

Early the next morning, I woke up to the whine of the big saw whirring its way through a log at the mill next door. I sat up in bed to discover my grandfather sitting at his desk at the other end of the porch.

"Good morning, Pepere," I shouted across the room. "What are you doing?"

My grandfather smiled that little smile of his. "Come here, and I'll show you."

In his hand, Pepere held a letter from the state property tax division.

"In Sinclair, we pay our property taxes directly to the State of Maine," he said. "I'm in arrears."

"Arrears?" I responded. "What's that?"

"I owe the state for two years," my grandfather said. "When Memere got sick I got a little behind. Now, the state wants its money."

My grandfather put the letter back on his desk and picked up another document. It was a proposed purchase agreement from an auto dealer in St. Agatha.

"This fellow in Saint-Ah-Gut wants to buy my car," my grandfather said. "It seems like a good deal, and I will still have my pick-up to drive around."

"Where's Saint-Ah-Gut," I asked. "I never heard of it."

My grandfather pointed in the general direction of the village. "It's about ten miles up the road at the other end of the lake."

I looked down at the letterhead on the sales agreement. I concluded that "Saint-Ah-Gut" and St. Agatha were the same place.

For breakfast, I had a glass of orange juice and ate a box of cereal. Mama had stuffed several little boxes of cereal into a paper shopping bag. I got lucky. I pulled out a box of Frosted Flakes. My mother used scissors to cut along the dotted lines to open one side of it. I poured in a little milk and ate the flakes right out of the box.

It was still early, but it was quite warm. I asked my mother if it was okay for Teddy and me to go for a swim.

"You have to wait an hour before you go in," she said. "You have to let your food digest."

While waiting for breakfast to "digest," my brother and I hung around the bungalow listening in on and trying to figure out what the three adults were saying to each other as they conversed in French.

When I did get the green light to go swimming, I was out the door like a shot. I ran down the banking to the lake and did a cannonball off the end of the dock. I swam around for a while in deep water without touching the bottom.

Teddy stood at the end of the dock watching me. "How is it?," he asked.

I cut through the water toward shore. When I got next to the dock, I stood up.

"Aw, shit," I said. I was up to my knees in muck. I reached down and came up with a handful of wet sawdust. I showed it to my little brother. "This stuff is a foot deep," I shouted. "It must come from that sawmill."

Still, I was bound and determined to swim. I turned around and launched myself back toward the deep water. I used the breaststroke, whipping my legs wide apart in an exaggerated motion in an effort to keep my feet from touching the bottom.

I swam around for about five minutes when I noticed my grandfather, a cigarette dangling from his mouth, standing next to Teddy on the wharf.

"I just come down to check on you boys," he explained in his gravelly voice.

I was glad to see Pepere. Sometimes, Papa would take us to public beaches in Sidney or Winthrop, but he never stayed around to watch us swim. He always struck out swimming on his own.

I put on a show for my grandfather, paddling around in a circle near the end of the dock.

"How do you like my swimming?" I yelled up to him.

Pepere watched for a moment.

"You swim like a frog," he said distinctly with hardly a trace of an accent. A little smile played at his lips. It felt nice to receive a compliment from him.

I swam around for a few minutes more before I found a way to crawl out of the water onto the wharf without touching the muck. My grandfather stayed until I got out of the water. After he went back into his bungalow, Teddy and I spent some time at the end of the dock basking in the sun. We sat with our legs dangling in the water; our feet far above the sawdust below.

When I went back indoors, Pepere and my father were embroiled in a heated discussion out on the porch. My father hovered over my grandfather, who sat at his desk.

At first, I didn't know what they were talking about.

The debate alternated between French and English.

When I heard my father angrily say "Chrysler," my grandfather calmly picked up a piece of paper and showed it to Papa. It was his tax bill.

Then Pepere handed him another piece of paper. It was the proposed sales agreement for the big blue sedan.

At this point, Papa saw me standing in the doorway. "Get lost," he barked. "Your grandfather and I are talking. It's man talk. Go find something else to do."

As usual, I did what I was told. I went back outside. I walked across the road, where I found a gruesome scene unfolding.

Butch's dad stood In the middle of the barnyard holding a hatchet in his right hand while pinning one of the chickens on a chopping block in front of him with his muscular left arm.

He brought the hatchet down with a powerful swing.

Thwack!

The headless chicken shot across the barnyard

Butch handed his father another chicken and stepped back.

Thwack!

The chicken ran without its head across the driveway toward the house.

Butch's dad stopped for a moment and looked at me.

"Hey, kid." He held up the hatchet. "You want to give it a try?"

"No, thanks." I shook my head. "Not today."

Butch's dad let out a hardy laugh before bringing the hatchet down again.

Thwack!

Another headless chicken took off like a rocket. This one headed toward the road.

I didn't know what to think. I had never seen anything like it. I was enthralled.

Thwack!

Thwack!

Thwack!

Three headless chickens headed off in three different directions. None of them ran around. They just darted in a straight line with their short wings flapping before dropping to the ground forty or fifty feet away from the wooden stump where Butch's father wielded his hatchet.

Butch sidled up beside me. "Do you know why the chickens run like that without their heads?" he asked.

"No." I looked up at him. "Why do they do that?"

"Because they don't have any brains," Butch giggled. He poked me in the ribs. "Get it?"

I didn't laugh.

When his father was finished, Butch went around pushing a wheelbarrow picking up the dead birds.

After watching the chickens get slaughtered, I went for a walk alone along the Shore Road.

I had walked perhaps a half-mile down the road away from town when I heard a soft feminine voice call out to me.

It was Yvonne. She was sitting on the front stoop of her house. "Hey boy," she said. "What's your name?"

I told her.

Yvonne spoke English with an accent I hadn't heard before. I liked the sound of it.

She motioned to me. "Come here." With her accent, it didn't sound quite like a command. It sounded more like an invitation. I walked over to her.

"What are you doing in Sinclair?" she asked.

I told her.

"Where are you from?"

I told her that, too.

"Augusta? I've never been to Augusta," she said. "I went to Bangor once but never to Augusta."

Then, Yvonne smiled at me. No girl had ever smiled at me like that before. It was disarming.

"Ma mere says I don't do well in the sun," she said. "It's hot outside. Let's go inside the house for a while."

I was mesmerized. "Sure."

Yvonne stood up, reached out to take my hand and led me through the front door. "My parents have gone to St. Agathe for the afternoon, so I'm alone," she explained. She pronounced the name of the town exactly the way my grandfather had earlier that morning. I followed her through the house to a wide, screened-in verandah overlooking the lake. We ended up sitting on a porch swing. I sat at one end of the wide settee and she sat at the other.

We chatted about ourselves.

We talked about foods we liked. Spaghetti was high on both of our lists.

We discussed the music we liked to listen to. Yvonne was upset Elvis had been drafted into the army. "They cut off all his beautiful hair," she lamented.

I told her about movies I'd seen. "We have to go down to Caribou to see a movie," she said. The winter before, her family made the trip south to see *Gigi*.

We talked about school. We were both entering seventh grade. Yvonne liked all her subjects, while I liked history the most.

As we talked, we discovered we had a lot in common.

Also as we talked, Yvonne gradually edged closer to me. Her bare legs soon rubbed against my bare legs.

"You know," she said softly. "I like boys."

"I heard that," I mumbled.

"Do you like girls?"

"I think I do."

Yvonne put her head on my shoulder for a few moments. She then looked up at me and gently pulled my face down toward hers. She kissed me.

I had kissed girls before, but not like this. Usually, it was a quick peck and a mashing of closed mouths for a few moments. This was different. After a couple of those kisses, Yvonne parted her lips. Gently, but insistently, she used her tongue to part mine. I felt the tip of her tongue touch the tip of mine. I could feel the texture of her lipstick on my lips. I could taste it.

It was a different kind of kiss. I wasn't sure whether I liked it, but I felt it all the way down to my toes.

I didn't spend much more time with Yvonne. After I left, I walked slowly down the road toward the bungalow thinking about what had just happened. I wondered whether it was ever going to happen again.

That evening as I sat at one end of the table next to Mama, she reached over and ran her fingers across my upper lip.

"Where did this lipstick come from?" she asked. She held her finger out in front of my face, and I saw a faint dab of pink on it.

I didn't know what to say. I felt my face grow crimson.

Before I could begin babbling an answer, Pepere interceded. "Looks like my grandson has met Yvonne," he said. I thought I saw him smile. "She likes boys."

Mama didn't smile. "She likes boys too much if you ask me," she stated. Then, looking directly at me, she added: "You stay away from her."

I nodded. "Yes, Mama."

"Oh, let the boy have his fun," my father chimed in from the other end of the table. "You're only young once."

My mother looked across the table at my father. "If you say so, but I still think he ought to be careful."

My father grunted.

Butch's mother had brought over a large chicken casserole. It was the main dish for our supper. My mother put a large portion of it on everyone's plate.

As I looked down at the chunks of white meat, all I could see were those headless chickens running around in Butch's barnyard. It just didn't seem right to eat one so soon after I had seen it killed.

"I don't think I'm hungry," I announced.

I started to get up from the table, but my father made it clear I was to eat supper right then.

"This is all there is," he said. "You eat now or you starve."

My grandfather started to say something, but my father shot him a look. Pepere remained silent.

"You eat what is served you," my father reiterated.

"Yes, Papa," I said sullenly.

I sat sulking as I picked at the large serving of the casserole my mother had piled onto my plate. I ate the carrots, the peas, the small pieces of celery and green peppers, and I managed to spoon up enough broth for a few decent mouthfuls. I didn't eat any of the chicken.

Early the next morning, our departure from Sinclair came suddenly without warning.

"Get up," my father said, as he rousted me out of bed. "We're going home. Get dressed and get your things out to the truck."

While I sat up and wiped the sleep from my eyes, I heard my mother plead with my father out in the kitchen.

"It's Sunday," she said. "What are we going to do about church? I thought we were all going to go to mass together."

I could tell from the tone of my father's voice that his mind was made up.

"Forget about that," he said. "We'll go to church along the way. We'll stop in Caribou or somewhere else and go to a late mass."

"What about breakfast?" Mama asked.

Papa had it all figured out. He always did.

"The boys can eat their cereal in the back of the truck," he answered. "You can give Belle her bottle. I'll pick up a box of donuts for us at the store in the village."

After quickly gathering my belongings and stuffing them into the gym bag, I headed out the door.

My father trailed right behind me with an armful.

"Your grandfather is a mean old sonofabitch," he sputtered. "He won't help us out with the car."

I knew he was talking about the Chrysler. My grandfather wouldn't sell him the sedan.

My father didn't elaborate. He never did.

I knew my father was wrong. Pepere wasn't "a sonofabitch." He was easy to be with, and fun. I liked him.

It was the first time I thought my father was wrong about anything.

Up until then, Papa's word had been Bible. The law.

From then on, everything he told me would be subject to scrutiny. And it was.

GIRL I LEFT BEHIND

SUMMER 1965

About a month before I joined the Army I met Millicent.

We didn't fall in love or anything like that, but we got to know each other really well during that brief span of time between my graduation from high school and my enlistment date. I was in a state of suspended animation, waiting to embark on the next phase of my life. As it turned out, Millicent was waiting for what came next, too.

We both worked at the First National Store in the new strip mall on Western Avenue in Augusta. Millicent was a pretty girl with short blonde hair and dark eyes. She worked as a cashier in the front of the store and I worked as a clerk in the meat and produce departments at the rear of the store. I didn't spend much time up near the cash registers, but I noticed Millicent, "the cute girl out front," as some of guys called her, right off. It was hard not to notice someone like her.

We didn't meet at work, however.

One night after the store closed, we began talking to each other while walking home. We took the same route; straight down Western Avenue, right onto Sewall Street and left onto Capitol Street. It was dark, and I didn't realize there was anyone walking ahead of me until I was in front of Jack's Cash Market. I caught up to Millicent when she stopped to wait for the light to change at the intersection of State and Capitol Streets near the Blaine House, home of Maine's governor.

"I hope you don't think I am following you," I said as we stood next to each other on the curb.

I could hear the song *Laugh Laugh* blaring from the open window of a car stopped on the street.

"Oh," she chuckled. "I didn't even know you were behind me. Lost in my own little world, I guess."

After the light changed and the car with The Beau Brummels crooning in it made the turn heading toward the west-side rotary, we quickly walked across State Street.

I was still in my work clothes, a white shirt and black necktie.

"I know who you are," she said when we reached the other side, her eyes lighting up as she playfully tugged on my tie. "You're the boy who never comes out from the back of the store."

"Nobody sees me if I can help it," I admitted.

"Ooh" she said. "A man of mystery. I like that."

I nearly blushed.

"I guess so," I said meekly.

Millicent barely came up to my shoulders, but her little body seemed to radiate warmth and energy. Everything she said came with a smile. I had never met anyone like her.

After standing on the street corner for a few more moments, we parted company. I continued walking down the sidewalk to the apartment where I lived with my mother, while Millicent crossed the street and disappeared into the darkness of Capitol Park.

Two nights later, we walked home together again after the store closed. Millicent learned that I had just turned eighteen, and I learned that she was nearly two years older than I was. While we walked, she told me she had moved down from Waterville to live with an aunt on Columbia Street on the opposite side of the park from where I lived.

Her aunt worked for the Internal Revenue Service, located in a red brick building on that side of the park.

"Aunt Cynthia is my favorite relative," she said. "She is tons of fun to be with. We do a lot of things together."

When Millicent first moved to Augusta, her aunt took her to see *The Sound of Music* at The Colonial Theater. "Julie Andrews was wonderful," she gushed, "and all of the Van Trapp kids were so cute."

I told Millicent I went with a carload of guys two weekends before to Manchester to see *For A Few Dollars More* at the drive-in. "We bought a couple of bags of Dawson beer at State Street News," I said. "Didn't drink enough to get drunk, though."

Millicent gently elbowed me in the ribs. "You're kind of young to be drinking beer, aren't you?" The legal drinking age in Maine was twenty-one.

As we walked on, I said, "I figure if I'm old enough to join the Army, I'm old enough to drink beer."

"You're joining the Army?" There was a hint of concern in her voice. "With a war going on in Vietnam?"

"What war?" I joked.

The quip went right over her head.

"Oh, c'mon," she said. "Surely, you know about the war?"

I became serious. "Of course, I know, but it's going to be different for me. I'm going to Army finance school. The recruiter said the Army is going to teach me how to push a pencil, not how to push a rifle. I'm going to help keep the books."

"Oh," she said. "A smarty pants."

"I don't know about that," I responded. "I just know I need to get out of here. I'm sick of everything here. I don't have the money to go to college. The Army's my ticket out of town."

It was the first time I told anybody about my reasons for joining the Army. It was odd that I should share that with someone I hardly knew, but I liked her interest.

"Do your father and mother know about how you feel?"

"I don't have a father," I told her. "I just have a mother."

That was the end of that conversation.

When I was very young, my mother told me my father died during World War II. As I got older and learned about procreation and periods of gestation, I did the math. The end of the war and the time of my birth didn't add up.

One day, shortly after I became a teenager, I asked my mother about the discrepancy.

"Did I say World War II?" she said, brushing it off. "I meant the Korean War. Your father died in the Korean War."

I was old enough to remember that war. On Saturday afternoons I sometimes walked downtown with some of the other little boys from the neighborhood to watch the matinee at the Capitol Theater. I recalled seeing newsreels about the Korean Conflict.

Back then, we lived in an apartment with her parents down on Gage Street close to the shoe shop where my mother worked. I didn't remember anyone else living with us then. What she told me about my father just didn't jibe. I was sure I would remember him if he had been around then.

After my mother and I moved into our own apartment on Capitol Street next to the park, she began shacking up with a series of men. One after another, they trickled in and out of our lives.

Her current beau was Phil, a truck driver who was out on the road three or four days at a time.

While Phil was gone, things went well between my mother and me, but the atmosphere changed as soon he returned from his long hauls and resumed his residence on the couch in the front room. My mother became a different person when Phil was home, and it was clear she didn't want me around. We didn't joke as much with each other. And Phil just about ignored me completely.

One time, I came home from school early and caught them snuggling together on the couch in the dark during the middle of the afternoon.

"What the hell are you doing here?" Phil asked. "Aren't you supposed to be working today?"

Laying under a blanket, my mother, who was supposed to be at work herself, clung to Phil like a vine. She didn't say a word.

I changed as quickly as I could and left. Even though I wasn't scheduled to work that day, I put on my white shirt and black tie. I spent the rest of the day walking around the park smoking cigarettes. I didn't come home until after dark.

The park had always been a refuge for me.

When I was younger, I played Cowboys and Indians or Hide-and-Seek in the woods near the monument at the end of the park furthest from the State House. During the summer, the boys from the surrounding neighborhoods would play baseball all day in the park. Then we'd go home, change into our uniforms and play in a boys' league that night on the diamonds over by the Naval Reserve Center.

In the fall, it was football. We'd use the park's two long rows of stately elms as yard markers.

Once, I played Run of the Arrow with one of the older boys from Child Street. We started near the monument. He shot an arrow into the air toward the State House, and a bunch of us kids took off running after it. When we passed his arrow, the big kid started running in the same direction. The object of the game was to get to the other end of the park before his next arrow did. I turned down an invitation to play that game again.

Later, much later, I put my hands on a girl's breasts for the first time behind that monument. We petted in the tall grass between the railroad tracks and a small grove of pine trees. That was as far as we went.

One night as we walked down Sewall Street after work, Millicent muttered, "Aw, shit! There he is again."

I followed her glance to an old Ford sedan slowly cruising down the street in the same direction we were walking.

"There is who again?" I asked.

"Nobody special," she said. "I'll tell you about it later."

The car turned left at the corner and headed toward State Street.

Ordinarily, it took me a little more than ten minutes to walk home from the First National. With Millicent walking by my side, it took a little longer. I wasn't in any hurry.

That night, we didn't part company on the street corner as usual.

That night, I went with her into the park, where we sat on a little metal bench at the base of the steep embankment right across the street from the State House.

It was there that Millicent told me the real reason she had moved in with her aunt.

"I'm going to have a baby," she announced.

"Wow," I said. "You mean, you're getting married."

"No, I'm not getting married. I'm pregnant."

I was quite surprised to hear this. She didn't look pregnant. A little plump maybe, but not pregnant.

"When?" I asked.

"Another four months."

Millicent paused.

I could tell she was wondering whether she should say anything more about the subject. She continued, "I came to Augusta to have the baby. My parents thought I should leave Waterville for a while."

Then Millicent told me about Bud, the driver of the old Ford sedan. "He broke up with me after I told him about the baby," she said.

After Millicent moved to Augusta, Bud began driving down from Waterville to see her. "He says he just wants to talk," she said, "but I think he just wants to have sex. That's all he's ever wanted from me."

Then Millicent told me what her mother and father said she ought to do. "My parents want me to give the baby up for adoption."

I sat in rapt silence. I really didn't know how to respond to these revelations.

Millicent continued, "My parents told me they'd help pay my way through business school. I don't want to spend the rest of my life working at the First National. I think I want to be like my aunt and be on my own."

I could relate to that.

"I know what you mean," I said. "I'm not crazy about that place either."

My work at First National was fairly humdrum, and it became even more so after I received my Army enlistment date. As the designated gopher in the meat and produce department, I cleaned the machines, pushed a broom, mopped the floor, toted around the heavy boxes and burlap bags that the fruit and vegetables came in and helped move around the sides of beef on delivery days.

One of my favorite tasks was making hamburg in the big walk-in cooler. I'd disappear for thirty minutes or so and use a large wooden mallet to force the meat, gristle and bones that had been trimmed from the various cuts of beef through a giant meat grinder.

I was the only high school student who worked in meat and produce. Most of the men and women who worked at the back of the supermarket were much older. I didn't have much in common with them.

When I was in the produce department, I worked a lot with a guy named Vic, who always seemed to have a cigarette dangling from his mouth when he was in back and out of sight of the shoppers.

Vic always called me kid. He'd say "Kid, why don't you trim the lettuce?" or "Kid, why don't you go out front and make room for more bananas? They're on sale this week." It was like he didn't know my name.

After Vic learned I was going to enlist in the Army, he seemed to take more of an interest in me. He told me he had served in the Army during World War II.

"Kid, make sure you always have plenty of Trojans with you," Vic said out of one side of his mouth. The stubby remains of a cigarette dangled from the other side of his lips as he groomed one head of iceberg lettuce after another. "You never know when you might need one. A good-looking fellow like you might need a lot of them."

Vic seemed to have sex on his mind a lot.

One day, he reached into a cardboard box with the word "Chiquita" stamped in big letters on its sides and pulled out a long banana.

"Hey Lucy, you wanna see me turn this banana into a peach?" he asked.

Lucy was a woman who worked in the produce department wrapping fruits and vegetables. A lot of the produce was wrapped in cellophane before it was put out on the floor for display. First National didn't want the customers to touch the merchandise.

Vic slid the banana under his white apron with one hand and performed some sort of incantation while the other hand hovered out in front of him. Moments later, it looked like he had a giant erection pressing against his apron.

"Ain't that a peach?" he asked.

Vic laughed so hard that he started to cough. Lucy turned her back to him and went back to wrapping. I guess she had seen that one before.

I was marking time, and as my enlistment date drew near, my hours at First National were cut back. I wasn't working as many evening shifts, which meant I wasn't able to walk home with Millicent as much, either.

I thought about walking up and meeting her at the store at the end of her shift, but that seemed too much like a date.

While I was in high school, I never went out on a date with a girl. I liked girls, a few of them quite a bit, but I was afraid of being shot down so I never asked any of them out. I didn't have a car and that put me at a disadvantage. Also, I gave a lot of the money I earned to my mother to help pay our expenses, so I didn't have much left to spend.

I hung out a lot at Market Square Lanes, a candlepin bowling alley in downtown Augusta. Sometimes I'd pick up a girl there and spend some time with her in the back seat of a buddy's car while we went parking up near the quarry on Granite Hill in Hallowell. A few times I ended up walking a girl home from dances at the YMCA, the gym at St. Mary's School or the roller rink on Augusta's east side. Along the way, we'd find a dark secluded place to fool around.

None of these spontaneous encounters ever got serious. None of them ever progressed beyond the fondling stage. I didn't consider them dates. They just happened.

The next time I walked home with Millicent we deviated from our normal routine. We stopped at Howard Johnson, the restaurant with the orange roof on Western Avenue across the parking lot from the First National.

It was a Friday night, and the booths and tables were filled, so Millicent and I sat on adjoining stools at the counter that curled around the front of the restaurant.

Millicent started off by thanking me. "I appreciate you not telling anyone about my predicament," she said. "I haven't told a soul at First National about the baby."

I shrugged. "I figured it wasn't anybody's business but yours. Besides, I don't gossip."

Millicent reached out and gently rubbed her fingers across the back of my hand as my arm lay on the countertop. "I appreciate that," she said.

When the waitress came, Millicent ordered a large hot fudge sundae. "I'm eating for two now," she whispered.

I ordered a cup of coffee with lots of cream and sugar. Phil, who was drafted into the Army after Korea, told me he drank a lot of coffee while he was in. I was trying to pick up the habit.

Millicent made a wry observation. "It's Friday night," she said. "Why is a nice-looking fellow like you having a cup of coffee with a pregnant gal at HoJo's? Don't you have a girlfriend?"

I shook my head. "Naw," I said. "I don't date."

"Don't you like girls?"

I nodded. "Of course, I do. I just haven't had much luck with them."

As we touched upon this subject, I felt a little constriction in my throat. I was getting nervous.

Millicent must have sensed how I was feeling. She touched my arm again. "Hey," she said. "I don't mean to embarrass you."

Her touch relaxed me.

"I guess I really don't know how to be with girls," I said. "One of my buddies told me once I either come on too strong or I don't come on strong enough. He said it was a matter of timing. I didn't know what he was talking about."

"He sounds like a smart guy." Millicent smiled as she squeezed my hand. "You should listen to him."

I told her about some of my experiences with girls.

"I used to see this girl at dances, and we'd spend the whole night dancing and then go our separate ways. I never even kissed her." I paused to sip from my mug. "I seldom saw her at school. We were never in the same classes. I liked her, I guess, but when I did see her in the hallway, I'd just say 'hi' and walk on. I usually had to be some place else."

As I talked, Millicent worked on her sundae. She started by neatly plucking the cherry off the top with her spoon. "They should put more cherries on their sundaes," she said. "I love cherries."

Then I told Millicent about another girl I liked.

"I used to call her and we seemed to have great conversations on the telephone," I said, "but I couldn't think of a thing to say to her when I saw her face-to-face at school. I never asked her out, and she ended up going steady with somebody else."

Millicent was scraping the bottom of her sundae, trying to collect the last bit of the hot fudge sauce when she stopped abruptly and grabbed my arm.

"We gotta go," she said. "He's here."

"Who's here?"

"It's him," she said. "Bud." When we stood up, Millicent clung to my arm. "Down at the far end of the counter."

As we walked around the counter, I saw a scrawny redheaded guy sitting on the last stool at the end of the counter. He didn't look much older than I was. He wasn't much taller than Millicent and I outweighed him by at least twenty-five pounds. I was surprised Millicent was having a baby with someone like him.

When we got to the register, which was right next to where Bud sat, I told Millicent to stand by the door while I paid the check. I tried to be cool. I pretended Bud was not there and focused all my attention on the girl at the register.

"Was everything all right, sir?" she asked.

"Everything's fine." I smiled at her and then I looked down, beaming at Bud, who glared back at me. "Thanks for asking."

Millicent and I walked in silence for the next ten minutes or so. Before we parted at the street corner where we had first spoken with one another, she reached up and hugged me. "Thank you for being there," she said.

Then she slowly walked away into the park's shadows.

After she left, I waited for several minutes. From where I stood, I could see long stretches of both State and Capitol. I was on the lookout for an old Ford sedan. When it didn't materialize, I walked home.

I worked one more evening shift before I left to join the Army.

That night, our walk ended with Millicent and me sitting on a park bench.

"You should be out with a girlfriend tonight, not with me," she said.

"Like I've been telling you, I've never had a girlfriend." Then I shook my head. "I can't really believe I'm talking to you about this stuff. I've never talked to a girl about this, not even my mother."

"I can't believe you've never been with a girl," Millicent said. "A good-looking boy like you shouldn't have any problem with girls."

I could feel my face redden.

"You sound just like that song," Millicent joked. Then she warbled, "You're just a lonely boy, lonely and blue."

"I'm not that lonely and I'm not blue," I responded.

Millicent started to move a little closer to me.

"Whoa, that feels funny," she said as she slid along the bench.

"What feels funny?"

"The baby," she answered.

I looked down at her belly. "Did the baby kick? I heard that babies kick."

Millicent reached out and took my hand. "It's not a kick. It's too soon." She guided my hand to her tummy. "It's more like a flutter, like a butterfly trying to get out." Millicent lifted her blouse. "Here," she said. "Feel." She sensed my reluctance. "Go ahead. Feel it."

I gently touched her slightly swollen belly. I was surprised by its firmness. I didn't feel anything flutter. All I could feel was the softness of her skin.

When I looked up at Millicent, her face was just inches from mine. In the dim light, I saw the serious look on it, and I noticed how her eyes seemed to sparkle.

"You're so sweet and cute," she said. "I really can't help myself."

Millicent leaned in and kissed me, really kissed me. We embraced, and we kissed again and again.

Everything happened so fast.

The next thing I knew we were down on the grass. My pants were pulled down and her skirt was hiked up. She was on top of me, and we were doing it on the ground right across the street from the State House steps.

I didn't keep track of time. It seemed to end way too quickly, but at the same time it seemed to last forever. It was the best feeling I'd ever had.

"There," Millicent said, as she sat straddling me. "What do you think of that?" She was still panting.

"Wow," I said, momentarily at a loss for words. "I didn't know anything could feel that good."

Millicent leaned over and kissed me.

"Yes," she said. "That felt very good. I had forgotten how good it can feel."

Even in the dim light, I could see the smile on her face.

That was the last time I walked home from work with Millicent.

Three days later, I took a bus to Portland and took the oath of enlistment with a half-dozen other guys at the Army Recruiting Center.

We flew to Newark on an old prop-driven Constellation with wings that seemed to flap. A long bus ride through the dark to south Jersey followed the flight.

We pulled into Fort Dix around midnight, but the Army never really sleeps. We spent about an hour at the supply depot. We were measured and sized and then we received our basic summer military issue. I stuffed it all into a large, olive-drab duffel bag that had my name and serial number stenciled on the side of it.

Next we were marched to some old wooden barracks, where we spent the next two days. We got a haircut, received a so-called "Flying Ten" dollar bill to buy toiletries and other personal care items at the PX, took more placement tests and met with a personnel specialist to start our military file. Mostly, we stood around in formation. Waiting.

Army life was an immediate shock to my system.

The drill instructors kept us hopping. Each day, we got up in the dark and went to sleep in the dark. We ran or marched everywhere. Some guys were slapped around. To avoid that, I learned to pay attention and to do what I was told. And I never asked for an explanation of what I was told. Early on, I saw what happened to those trainees who sought further clarification of orders they had just been given.

In rapid succession, I learned how to disassemble an M-14 rifle and then reassemble it, how to shoot and clean it, how to throw a hand grenade and use a gas mask, and, in an introduction to first aid, how to treat a sucking chest wound.

Every Wednesday afternoon just before chow, the company clerk held mail call out in the parking lot in front of our barracks. Attendance was mandatory.

At the first few mail calls, I didn't get any letters. I wasn't expecting mail. I didn't write anyone. I was too busy, it seemed. So I was shocked when the clerk called out my name at a mail call about five weeks into the training cycle.

The letter was scented with perfume. It was from Millicent. She had received my address from my mother. She wrote to see how I was doing and to tell me how she was. She still didn't know what she was going to do about her baby and was having second thoughts about giving it up for adoption.

"I thought I wanted to be like my aunt and not get married or have children," she wrote, "but now I'm not so sure. If I keep the baby, I know

I won't be able to lead my life like my aunt does. I know the baby would come first."

Millicent said she had started to talk with Bud.

"He seems to be more concerned now about me and my baby," she wrote. "He has promised to stand by me and our baby. That is all I can ask of him, I guess. But I still don't know what I'm going to do."

She also said I had scared Bud the night he saw us together at the restaurant. "He was afraid he was going to lose me to you forever," she said. "He didn't want that to happen."

In her letter, Millicent made no mention of our encounter in the park.

Before she signed off, she wrote: "Let me know how you're doing."

That weekend, I wrote Millicent. In the letter, I listed some of my adventures at basic training. I told her we had just finished spending a week on the firing range and we were now getting ready to go on bivouac and spend a week camping out in tents.

I didn't offer any advice about her quandary but I did wish her luck.

I didn't say anything about what happened the last time we saw each other. After five weeks of basic training it seemed like that had happened to someone else, anyway.

I didn't receive another letter from Millicent.

A couple of days after I returned home on leave following basic training, I wore my khakis to see Vic in the produce department at First National. He was impressed. "You look good in that uniform, kid. Looks like the Army has already put some muscle on you."

Vic was right. I started basic training at a stocky one hundred seventy-five pounds. I came out of it eight weeks later at exactly the same weight, but it had been rearranged. I was now broader in the shoulders and trimmer in the waist.

I asked Vic about Millicent.

"She just up and quit is what I heard," he said. "Did you know she was pregnant?" He put both of his hands out in front of his stomach. "Last time I saw her she was right out to here."

Later that afternoon, I walked across the park to Columbia Street. I looked for the return address on the envelope containing Millicent's letter. It was the rear apartment of a duplex located next to the Internal Revenue Service's parking lot.

The flat looked empty.

I was staring through a window into the kitchen when an old man appeared holding a broom and a dustpan.

He opened the door.

"Can I help you, soldier?"

"Yeah," I said. "What happened to the people who lived here?"

The old man looked in the direction of the IRS building. "Uncle Sam gave the woman a promotion," he said. "She moved to Massachusetts."

I had more questions.

"What about her niece, Millicent? Did she move with her?"

"Nope." The old man shook his head. "She left a couple of weeks ago. I guess she went home. She was getting ready to have a baby, you know."

I nodded. "Yeah, I knew that."

I never saw Millicent again.

I never found out what happened to her.

I also never forgot her.

Claymore Mine

January 1967

It was the most vivid dream I ever had. I was out at the Windsor Fair on a Saturday night. Or maybe it was the Fourth of July over in Capitol Park in Augusta. Or on the beach at Lake Maranacook across the street from the American Legion post in Winthrop. Somewhere, someone was setting off fireworks.

I rarely dreamed in Technicolor, but I could see the bright plumes of light exploding in the night sky. It was so real that I could hear the shouts of men running around in the dark setting off the sparklers. I could hear the *pffft* as the canisters left the tubes and the muffled *whomp* as the colorful plumes suddenly blossomed.

My dream ended abruptly when one of my bunkmates rushed in through the doorway of our barracks.

"Two weeks to go, and Charlie is trying to kill me," he bawled as he started to rummage through his wall locker.

"Who is Charlie?" I asked. I wasn't fully awake.

"You know!" he screamed, stopping his frantic search for a moment. "The VC! The Viet Cong! The NVA! They're all trying to kill me!"

Pffft. Slight pause. *Whomp.*

"Where the hell did I put that thing?" He turned to me. "Have you seen my rifle?"

"It's there," I said, pointing to the M-14. It hung by its shoulder strap from the bedpost at the end of his bunk.

After grabbing the rifle, my roommate left as quickly as he had arrived.

Now I knew exactly what happened. As I slept, my subconscious had tried to make sense of the *pfffts* and the muffled *whomps* that followed them. My subconscious was wrong. It wasn't fireworks. It was mortar rounds. I wasn't back in Maine. I was at a U.S. Army base at Phu Bai in the Republic of South Vietnam, and we were under attack.

Suddenly, a siren verified that fact.

Since my arrival at the radio research station nearly a year before, we had had a dozen or so simulated drills. Over and over again, mostly in the dead of night, we practiced how we would respond in such situations. We had never been hit before, but I knew exactly what I was supposed to do.

I dressed as fast as I could. After putting on my ammo belt and steel pot, I slung the small cloth pouch containing the claymore mine over my shoulder, grabbed my M-14 and headed out the door.

Not every soldier on our post carried a Claymore during alerts. I was given one of the mines the day I reported for duty at Phu Bai.

It wouldn't have been my first choice. I would have liked to have manned an M-60 machine gun in one of the sandbagged bunkers, where I would be less exposed. I had fired that belt-fed automatic weapon during the Tactical Training Course at Fort Devens in Massachusetts just prior to shipping out to South Vietnam. It rocked.

The M-60 was more of an offensive weapon, while the Claymore was a weapon of last resort to be fired only after Viet Cong or North Vietnamese Army troops had penetrated our perimeter.

Before I set it off, a lot had to happen. First, the marauders would have to hack their way through five yard-wide coils of concertina wire. Then, they would have to thread their way through the 30,000 anti-personnel mines seeded within a 50-yard-wide swath around the post. Next, they would have to climb over the two eight-foot-high, barbed wire fences that surrounded the post and advance through the 75-yard-wide killing zone in front of the trench line.

All these hurdles had to be surmounted while the attackers received withering fire from hundreds of American soldiers armed with semiautomatic rifles, grenade launchers and a variety of machine guns.

Less than a minute after my dream ended, I stepped out of the long pre-fab metal trailer that served as the B Company barracks. No sooner had my feet hit the ground when a mortar round exploded up the street no more than fifty yards to my left, near the north end of the mess hall.

From the large plume of sparks, I could tell it was a white phosphorus round. *Willy Peter.* I didn't stop to watch it burn. I also didn't think about where the next round was going to land. I didn't have time. I sprinted in a straight line as fast as I could to the trench line about a hundred yards away.

I found my position inside the trench, the exact spot I always went to during the practice alerts. Leaving my rifle behind, I crawled out of the trench and ran forward in a low crouch to deploy the Claymore. I got lucky. It was a moonless night, but I quickly found the small pile of sandbags about fifty feet in front of the trench. After a few seconds of groping around with my hands, I found the concrete block embedded in the front of the mound.

I removed the Claymore from its pouch, slid it into a slot facing away from the post and attached two electrical leads to the device. Then I ran back to the trench, uncoiling the wire as I went. After dropping into the five-foot cut, I attached the wire to the pistol-grip magneto. The Claymore was now armed.

I had been warned about not attaching the magneto to the wires until I was a safe distance from the mine. "There is one helluva back blast," my instructor had stressed when he showed me how to deploy and arm the mine. "You don't want to be close to this thing when it goes off."

A Claymore contained thousands of tightly packed beads of metal embedded into a half-pound of C-4. The explosive was encased in an inch-thick, slightly curved, gray plastic-covered block that measured about eight inches in length and five inches in width. All I had to do was to press the trigger on the magneto to launch lethal, supercharged grapeshot in a 180-degree arc in front of my position.

Dozens of soldiers along the trench line that ran for more than a mile around the post had done what I did. They had placed the Claymores they had carried, creating an interlocking field of fire around the entire perimeter with the deadly devices.

After the rude awakening, the mad dash to the trench line and the deployment of the Claymore, my adrenaline was pumping. In a matter of a few minutes, I had gone from being dead to the world to being as alive as I had ever been. If I was scared, I didn't know it. I was too excited.

The explosions moved in a southerly direction away from the post. A few minutes more and the *pffffts* stopped completely. There were no more *whomps*. A deathly silence ensued.

"Do you think they're coming tonight?" It was Anderson, the fat guy from the Comm Center who I seldom saw in between trips to the trench line during alerts. "Do you think Charlie's going to try to overrun us?" There was real concern in his voice.

"I don't know." I slid an ammo clip into my rifle, leaned over the earthen parapet and peered into the darkness to our front. "But we've got to be ready."

I had wondered when the Viet Cong were going to get around to us. The 8th Radio Research Station was an important cog in the collection of communications intelligence. It had already received two Meritorious Unit Commendations for its work.

I was one of dozens of young soldiers at the 8th who performed primary traffic analysis. We scanned sheets and sheets of radio intercept looking for clues of the enemy's intentions.

Maybe tonight the VC was going to shut us down. It had already tried to hit us once before. A few months before, a squad of marines on patrol in the jungle just beyond the outer perimeter of the military installations at Phu Bai had discovered rocket-launching sites under construction more than a mile away from our post. They calculated the trajectory of the weapons and learned that the rockets were zeroed in on the operations center where I worked.

Accuracy wasn't an important element in a mortar attack. It was supposed to harass and disrupt. It did. The shelling lasted only a few minutes, but it forced the evacuation of the operations center for several hours, temporarily knocking us out of business.

A Marine once told me a good mortar man could put at least a dozen rounds into the air before the first one landed. A mortar tube sits on a bipod connected to a round metal base plate. As the mortar rounds are fired, the rear of the base plate is driven a little deeper into the ground by the recoil as the propellant blasts each round out of the tube. Each time the weapon is fired, the angle of the tube in relation to the ground widens and the trajectory of succeeding rounds grows sharper. In this way, the gunner can walk the mortar rounds back toward him.

The VC firing team had started its mortar attack at the north end of the post and walked its rounds south.

While we waited for the all-clear signal to sound, Anderson monitored the communication line inside a nearby sandbagged bunker. He listened in on a field phone, part of a network activated every time we went on alert. It was through this line that I would receive the order to fire the Claymore.

About a half hour after the attack, it was reported that two Korean contract workers were critically injured when a mortar round hit the large concrete water tank next to the mess hall.

"That must have been the round I saw go off," I told Anderson. I described what it looked like. "I guess nobody told those poor bastards what to do in case of a mortar attack. They shouldn't have been there, should they?"

It was a rhetorical question. He didn't answer it.

Later, Anderson heard that one of the last mortar rounds the VC fired hit a hooch housing a squad of Navy SeaBees just south of the compound. "None of them got out alive," he said.

I was shocked. "Jesus, I bet I knew some of those guys," I said. A squad of SeaBees from Davisville, Rhode Island, took the escape and evasion course with us at Fort Devens. "It's just a matter of luck, isn't it?"

Then Anderson heard a report that Marines stationed in a bunker on the outer perimeter had observed Viet Cong firing a mortar from inside Phu Bai village. Located less than a kilometer south of our compound, the area was designated a no-fire zone. The two or three Marines in the bunker had to wait for permission to abandon their post before they could chase the firing team out of there. By the time they were able to move, the VC had left.

"No-fire zone?" I said to Anderson. "What the fuck is that? What the hell are we doing here?"

Another rhetorical question. Anderson remained mum.

Less than two hours after the mortar attack had ended, a propeller-driven plane flew overhead. I couldn't see it, but I could hear it. It turned out to be *Puff The Magic Dragon*, an old DC 3 fitted with a battery of electronically fired machine guns capable of spraying thousands of rounds per minute on a target. I heard the plane move off to the southwest. I couldn't hear the sound of gunfire, but I did see a thick shaft of light switching off and on, piercing the darkness, as the air crewmen fired their guns.

Anderson noticed it, too. "I wonder what they're firing at?" he asked.

"Hopefully, it wasn't anybody we know," I answered. "*Puff* is supposed to have sensors on board. He can see in the dark. Whoever was down there isn't there anymore."

We spent another two hours out in the trenches.

The communications link was silent for most of that time.

"You think the colonel's over at the Officers' Club soaking up suds with his staff?" Anderson asked.

"I don't think officers are allowed to drink beer," I said. "I think they are restricted to Chivas Regal."

Along about daybreak, the all clear was issued.

While the other soldiers began drifting back to the barracks, I detached the wires from the magneto and climbed out of the trench to retrieve the claymore.

It was the first time in several hours I could let my mind wander.

As I began to roll up the wire, I thought about the men on the VC firing team who had lobbed the mortar rounds at us. I wondered what it felt like to feed those rounds into a mortar tube and fire them at someone you didn't know.

I wondered whether I could do that. Maybe next time I'd find out. Maybe next time I'd get a chance to set off my Claymore.

Maybe.

BUCK SERGEANT

JUNE 1967

It had taken us nearly eighteen hours of stop-and-go flying to make the 320-mile trip south from Phu Bai. We hopped from Phu Bai to Danang to Pleiku to Nha Trang and finally to the 22nd Replacement Battalion in Cam Ranh Bay. It was after four in the morning when we finally cleared customs and looked for empty racks in the barracks on the other side of the unit's sandy parade ground.

I didn't plan to pretend to be somebody else while waiting for my flight home from South Vietnam, but it seemed like a good idea at the time. As soon as we stepped into one of the makeshift barracks after traveling from the 8th Radio Research Field Station in Phu Bai, Sergeant P suggested I look into the large wooden box of worn-out uniforms at the far end of the barracks. All sorts of military clothing had been discarded by troops heading back to the States.

"Look for a fatigue shirt with sergeant stripes," Sergeant P instructed. "I don't know how long we're going to be here, but life will be much easier for you as an NCO."

I was a Specialist Fourth Class, one pay grade below a noncommissioned officer. As a Spec 4, I was a candidate for a variety of work details, but after spending twelve intense months working in a communications intelligence operations center, I needed a break before I reported for my next assignment. I just wanted to go home.

Rummaging around, I found an olive-drab shirt with three chevrons on its sleeves. It was faded but still serviceable. The nametag said the fatigue blouse belonged to a buck sergeant named Bennett. I held it up to show Sergeant P.

"Looks like I'm going to have to start calling you, Sergeant B," he said, throwing me a snappy salute. "Welcome to the club."

Less than three hours later, following a brief sleep, I tested Sergeant P's theory while standing at attention among a hundred soldiers in the mandatory morning formation. Immediately, about thirty soldiers were marched off to the mess hall. As I started to step off with them the master sergeant in charge of the formation called out to me: "Not you, sarge! You don't have to pull KP."

The ruse worked. Rank did have its privileges. A buck sergeant isn't much, but hardly anybody in the Army messes with an NCO, no matter how low he is on the totem pole.

I met Sergeant P about four months after I joined the Army. We were taking a course in traffic analysis at the United States Army Security Agency Training Center at Fort Devens in Massachusetts. I was a teenager just out of high school. In his early 30s, he was a seasoned veteran who had just signed up for his third six-year hitch. Sergeant P became a mentor of sorts. He was no great shakes as a traffic analyst, but he seemed to know all the ins and outs of Army life. Or so I thought.

Twenty-six soldiers were in our TA class when we started. As a joke, we started calling each other by a letter in the alphabet. That was how Sgt. P got his name. Our instructors were unaware of our private code, but it symbolized the highly classified nature of our work.

The ASA was the Army's signals intelligence branch. We required a top-secret crypto clearance to work inside an operations center. The security agency's unofficial motto was "In God We Trust; All Others We Monitor." The ASA tried to keep tabs on the Soviets and the Red Chinese and their allies at listening posts throughout the world.

Soldiers in the security agency were supposed to be among an extremely select group, the Army's so-called "top 10 percent." In fact, we were recruited from those soldiers who scored among the top two percent in the Army's aptitude tests. It was an all-volunteer outfit. Initial enlistment was for four years rather than the customary three years the other volunteers served.

Sergeant P's test scores didn't matter. He got dibs for assignment to an ASA unit as a reward for signing up for another hitch.

In Vietnam, we didn't serve in ASA units. It was supposed to be a covert operation. Instead, we were assigned to radio research outfits. Our units were provided with an elaborate, vaguely worded cover story that said we were involved in the study of the propagation of radio waves.

The rest of the Army really didn't know what to make of us or exactly what we did. Playing the role of a buck sergeant while at the 22nd seemed to be a logical extension. I was definitely working undercover.

At that point, when Sergeant P suggested I might try a new role, I was so close to leaving South Vietnam I could taste it. I was on an emotional high. I had survived my year in Nam, and I was going home. I could do no wrong.

I spent my first day at the replacement catching up on my sleep. That night, after taking a cold shower, I accompanied Sergeant P to the mess hall. We sat across from each other at a table in the rear of the dining area in a special section reserved for NCOs.

"Where are you guys from?" said a young staff sergeant as he sat down with his tray next to us.

I let Sergeant P do the talking. In keeping with my intelligence training, I listened.

"We were up in I Corps," Sergeant P said. He didn't reveal our unit's exact location.

"I Corps? Isn't that Marine country?"

Sergeant P nodded.

"What the hell were you doing way up there?" the staff sergeant asked.

"Can't tell you," Sergeant P said. "If I did, I'd have to kill you." He sounded serious.

The staff sergeant tried to smile. "Ohhh," he said. "I know what you guys are. A couple of spooks, aren't you? Sneaky Petes."

Sergeant P signaled we were done eating by pulling away from the table and standing up. Before we left the table he leaned over toward the staff sergeant. "You never saw us," he said in a low voice. "We were never here."

The staff sergeant nodded. "I get it," he said. "You were never here."

"You laid it on kind of thick, didn't you?" I said as we walked out of the mess hall.

"What he doesn't know won't hurt him," Sergeant P responded.

I wondered about that.

"Besides he'll spread the word and nobody will want to mess with us," Sergeant P added.

While many of the other low-ranking enlisted men spent their time at the replacement center pulling various work duties, I kept my head down. I spent the first couple of days at a little snack bar I found just down the road from the 22nd. I was killing time. There, I went through three Ian Fleming paperbacks someone had left behind in the barracks. In quick succession, I read about James Bond's exploits in *Moonraker*, *From Russia With Love* and *Dr. No.* It was good escape literature, but those stories were much better with a movie sound track.

I spent my dwindling supply of military script buying water buffalo burgers and Coca Cola. Grilled to perfection by the chubby petite Vietnamese woman who ran the place, the burgers were thick and juicy while the soda was much sweeter than what was bottled stateside.

I also fed a steady stream of coins into the jukebox. Over and over again, I listened to *Sunshine Superman*. I was so full of myself at that point I thought Donovan was singing about me. Every time the song came on I'd smile at the woman behind the counter, and she'd smile back. She had no idea what that song was about. Neither did I.

My time at the 22nd was quiet and peaceful. Located on the leeward side of a narrow peninsula, it was far enough away from the flight line so I couldn't hear the planes take off or land. It almost was like there wasn't a war there.

One day at the snack bar I talked about the lack of noise to Private First Class Whitney, a mechanic who worked up the road at the replacement battalion's motor pool. "I can't believe how quiet this place is," I told him. "Up north, where I was, there was always something popping off. A mortar round. Outgoing artillery. A machine gun in the distance. Always something."

The mechanic, his oily fingers wrapped around a burger, told me a regiment of South Korean troops was assigned to provide security on the outer perimeter. ROK troops patrolled the area at the top of the peninsula.

"The Koreans don't take no shit," he said. "They shoot first, and then they shoot again. I've heard they've wiped out entire villages when the VC has screwed with them." I felt safe but not safe enough to stay in South Vietnam.

At the following morning's formation, the master sergeant assigned six men to clean a latrine. I stood next to them in the same row of troops. Then, he looked at me. "Hey sarge, do me a favor. Could you take charge of these guys? Make sure they get rid of that crap."

No way was I going to get on the wrong side of this noncom. "No problem," I said. Off I went to lead the small squad of soldiers.

At the 8th RRFS, we had flush toilets and urinals in the barracks, both service clubs and the operations center, but this was a dry tenholer for the enlisted men. Soldiers sat on a wooden seat and took their dumps into the large metal laundry tubs below. If they had to, they peed into the ground through four-inch PVC tubes that were located in a separate enclosure.

After ordering two of the soldiers to haul one of the tubs out from under the building, it was obvious to me how to proceed.

I pointed to the soldier standing closest to me. "Come with me," I said in a commanding voice. "I want the rest of you guys to close the latrine and pull all the tubs out into the open away from the building."

I walked across the road to the motor pool, where I found PFC Whitney under the grease rack lubricating the fittings on a deuce-and-a-half truck.

"I need a can of gas," I told him. "Can you help me out?"

A few moments later, I walked back across the street to the latrine. I carried a handful of greasy rags in one hand, and the soldier who was with me toted a two-and-a-half gallon can of ethyl in his hands.

The tubs had been placed about six feet away from the building. None of them was anywhere near filled to capacity. I went around dousing their contents with liberal amounts of gasoline.

Then, I borrowed a cigarette lighter from one of the soldiers, ignited a rag and tossed it into one of the tubs. *Poof.* A few flames. A cloud of smoke. In less than a minute, the waste was reduced to ashes. I repeated the process until every tub was rid of its contents.

The entire operation took less than twenty minutes. "As far as I'm concerned this mission is accomplished," I told the soldiers. "You guys can have the rest of the day off."

I spent my final night at the 22nd at the NCO club with Sergeant P. We sat with some of the cadre from the replacement battalion, including the master sergeant who had assigned me to the shit detail earlier that day. We were celebrating our impending departure. The next afternoon, Sergeant P and I were scheduled to fly to the States on a chartered flight.

While Sergeant P held court at one end of the table, I maintained a low profile and sat slightly apart from the others at the other end.

Presently, a sergeant first class sidled up to the empty chair next to me. "Is this seat taken?" he asked.

"It's yours, sarge," I said.

I did a double take when he sat down.

"Any relation to Wild Bill?" I asked, pointing to the nametag on his jungle fatigues. It said HICKOK.

SFC Hickok grinned slightly. "As you know, Wild Bill met with an untimely demise," he said. "I don't think he had any progeny. His line ended with him, I believe." He sounded deathly serious.

Hickok was an artilleryman. With his erudite manner, he sounded more like a college professor. To me, his slight build and dark-rimmed glasses made him look more like an accountant or a bank teller.

Hickok had a gentle manner. While the NCOs at the other end of the table regaled each other with one tall tale after another, Hickok was content to sit in quiet conversation with me.

Vietnam was Wild Bill's third war. His artillery unit had come ashore in France three days after D-Day. Early in the Korean Conflict, his outfit had been in the Pusan Pocket. More recently, he had been based in South Vietnam's central highlands with a battery of 155-millimeter howitzers firing one hundred pound shells into the jungle up to ten miles away. All of this information came out during my friendly interrogation of him. I'd ask a question, and he would answer it.

My father had been a member of the so-called "brown shoe army" and had been an artilleryman during World War II. He had fought in the Battle of the Bulge. And here was Hickok, who was about my father's age, still doing it. It felt pretty cool being around him. I felt like I was at war with my dad.

Hickok didn't share his feelings about this war. We didn't have that type of conversation. He was waiting to catch a flight to Hawaii for five days of R & R, and he was more concerned about that.

"My wife is flying out from Kansas to meet me," he said. "Both of my daughters are in high school, and they've still got classes, so this will be like a second honeymoon." As we chatted, I wondered how such a mild-mannered man had managed to survive while seeing all that combat during his long military career.

Sometime after nine o'clock, I felt hungry. The mess hall was closed, so I asked Hickok if he wanted to go get a burger with me at the snack shack.

While we had been in the NCO club, a dense fog had drifted in from the South China Sea, which was no more than a mile-and-a-half away to the east. A heavy mist now shrouded the camp. It was a dark moonless night. Visibility was down to mere inches.

As we walked along the road toward the snack bar, we literally ran into two soldiers who were walking toward us from the opposite direction.

"You owe me an apology, soldier," one of them said as he warded me off with his hands.

I pushed back. "Hey," I said. "*You* ran into us."

"Keep your hands off a superior officer, soldier," his friend commanded. "We're both lieutenants."

Close up, neither one of them seemed any older than I was. In the dense fog, I couldn't make out any insignia. I didn't know what rank they were.

"Aw, bullshit," I said. "You guys are not officers."

We exchanged more shoves.

I felt a surge of adrenaline. I had Wild Bill and his cloak of invincibility next to me. I was sure we were more than a match for these two young soldiers. Then I took a look and discovered Hickok was no longer by my side. Now I realized his key to survival in combat.

I was alone, but it didn't make any difference. I was David. I was ready to take on *two* Goliaths. Besides, both of them seemed much drunker than I was.

The soldier nearest me tried to strike first, but he staggered as he sent a long looping right in my direction. I ducked off to my left and, as he was losing his balance, shoved him hard to the ground. When he went down, his boots got tangled up in the legs of his companion, who began to wobble and lose his own balance. I reached out and grabbed his shirt with both hands and threw him as hard as I could on top of his friend.

At that point a light went on in my brain. Uh-oh. Am I in trouble? Did I just assault two Army officers? That was serious business. Punishment was no slap on the wrist with an Article 15. It was a court martial offense.

Wild Bill was right. It was time to take off. I ran in the direction I had come from. Seconds later, when I was sure I had disappeared into the fog, I veered sharply toward the company area and got lost.

I never saw the two young officers — at least that is who they claimed to be — nor Hickok again. I didn't tell Sergeant P about the skirmish.

Later that night, as I lay sober in my rack trying to get some sleep while worrying whether a squad of MPs was about to descend upon me,

I thought about what had happened in the fog. I also thought how I had been conducting myself since my arrival at the replacement battalion. I realized my give-a-shit attitude could get me in a good deal of trouble.

A case of premature celebration is what it was. I was so excited about going home I had forgotten who I was, where I was and what I was supposed to be doing. I was still in the Army. I had nearly two more years to go before my enlistment was up. I couldn't forget that.

Before I fell asleep, I put the fatigue shirt with the buck sergeant chevrons on its sleeves back where I found it. From then on I would be a good trooper. I was going to walk the straight and narrow.

The next morning, as I was hurrying across the parade ground to catch the bus to the air base dressed in my tropical khakis and toting my duffle bag on one of my shoulders, a staff sergeant from the replacement battalion stopped me. The night before, he'd been among Sergeant P's drinking buddies at the NCO club.

"You know, someone could get in a world of hurt impersonating an NCO," he said sternly. He pointed at the Spec Four eagle emblem on my short-sleeved khaki blouse. "I looked it up. Dishonorable discharge. Loss of pay. Six months in the stockade."

Suddenly, I was unsteady on my feet. The air was sucked from my lungs. I was sure I was about to faint.

Then, the staff sergeant's expression changed.

"Don't let it happen again," he smiled. "Get out of here. Go home to the land of the big PX and find yourself a round-eyed woman."

He didn't say another word. He didn't have to. He had scared the shit out of me. Catching my second wind, I sprinted to the bus for my ride to the air base and my flight home.

SWEET WILLIAM

AUGUST 1969

Tom Webb and I sat in the corner of the little servicemen's club up near the parade ground at Fort Dix. Nearly two years had passed since we had last seen each other. Our paths had crossed at the 8th Radio Research Field Station in Phu Bai as I was nearing the end of my twelve-month stint in Vietnam.

Running into Spider, as he was called due to his surname and his tall, lanky build, was not an unusual occurrence. During my four years in the army, I often ran into someone I knew or someone who knew someone I knew. The world is smaller than we think.

The first time it happened I was standing in a line clutching my 201 file at the overseas replacement center in Oakland, California, when the soldier in front of me turned around and said "Hi." It was Fabrizio. A few months before, I had gone through basic training with him at Fort Dix. He had been in my company.

Both of us were on our way to Vietnam to serve as replacements with very different types of military units. Fabrizio was an 11B20, a rifleman, and I was a 98C20, a traffic analyst. He had been taught how to kill the enemy, and I had been taught how to analyze the enemy's radio transmissions. We really didn't have an opportunity to talk during that encounter. The Army quickly moved us along, and we went our separate ways.

Less than a week later, while waiting to board a plane at Tan Son Nhut Airport outside Saigon, I ran into Miscavage, another soldier from my basic training company. He had become a personnel clerk who spent a lot of his time setting up Rest and Recreation flights for the troopers from the First Cavalry.

"I have to come to Saigon two or three times a month." Miscavage smiled. "It's real rough duty."

Nearly ten months later in early 1967, as I sat in a quiet bar in Taipei while on my own R&R, a lone figure stood up from a table at the far end of the room and made his way over to me. It was Fabrizio.

He told me about his life as a grunt. "I've never walked so much in my life. I carry my rifle everywhere I go and I haven't had to fire it once. I just walk."

I couldn't tell Fabrizio what life was like for me in Vietnam. My work was classified. But also, after hearing his story, I was kind of embarrassed by my seemingly meager contributions to the fight. Besides, it would probably bore him.

This time, at Fort Dix, the huge military base in south New Jersey, I had encountered Webb. The first time I met Spider he had just arrived in Phu Bai after spending nearly a year in West Germany copying Morse code at Herzo Base. "Too much military bullshit," Webb had said then, explaining why he put in for the transfer to Vietnam. We sat next to each other in one of the radio intercept bays in the operations center waiting for a control station to come up. "They wanted us to wear starched fatigues all the time. Like that was going to make you take code any better."

I knew the drill. After Vietnam, I spent nearly two years in West Berlin at an Army Security Agency listening post built atop a mountain of rubble that had been piled in the heart of the city after World War II. It wasn't as tough as serving as a rifleman in the Berlin Brigade, where the infantrymen seemed dressed for a parade every day of the week. They even wore white gloves when they pulled guard duty.

The soldiers in my Berlin unit were supposed to pay special attention to their appearance, too. Apparently, the ASA wanted us to look as spiffy as we could while we carried out the top-secret functions of monitoring the radio and electronic communications of the Soviet Union and its East European affiliates.

As we gabbed in the intercept bay while waiting for the next *sked* to come up, I took in that a cigarette dangled from Spider's mouth, his dog tags hung loosely down the front of his dyed-green t-shirt, and he wore his headset curled around his neck. "Here at Phu Bai, at least I can breathe," he coughed, sending a large cloud of smoke swirling above his head.

The North Vietnamese military had undergone a major communications change, and it was my job to help recover some of the networks we had lost. Experienced "ditty boppers," as the radio intercept operators like to be called, were essential in helping traffic analysts like me. Webb had been in country for just a short time, but it was long enough for him to recognize the distinctive fist of the North Vietnamese radio operators he'd been monitoring. The singular way each one keyed his radio set while transmitting the dits and dahs of international Morse code was like the inking of a fingerprint.

For a couple of weeks, I took up residence in the intercept bay scanning the radio traffic as the ditty boppers typed it out on six-ply paper. I was looking for clues. I was trying to find the call signs and radio frequencies used by the North Vietnamese Army units with which I was responsible for "maintaining continuity." That was the term used over and over again by our instructors at Fort Devens. I was due to rotate to my next duty station. I was then a twenty-year-old whiz kid, and I wanted to recover all of my networks before I left.

Six months later while in West Berlin, I received a Certificate of Achievement, signed by General Westmoreland no less, thanking me for my work in support of counterinsurgency efforts against Communism in the Republic of Vietnam. Westy probably had no idea what I did, exactly. Even he didn't have a need to know everything.

It was a lazy Sunday afternoon at Fort Dix. Spider and I had the club almost to ourselves. The small bar was housed in an old single-story wooden building, one of those supposedly temporary structures put up when the military base was expanded before the start of World War II.

A couple of staff sergeants from the training brigade sat drinking at the bar. The sounds of Otis Redding, The Supremes, Marvin Gaye, and The Temptations emanated from the other end of the room. The two drill instructors had control of the jukebox. We weren't going to insert a coin into the slot. It was their club.

Webb and I weren't bosom buddies, but we did spend some time together in the same place, and when that place is Vietnam, it counts for something. We had some catching up to do.

The strange thing is we found that we'd spent the previous fifteen months in relatively close proximity to each other. While I was in West Berlin, Spider had returned to Herzo Base, just north of Nuremberg in Bavaria, to finish his hitch in the Army.

"I missed the beer, blintzes and babes," he explained. "Not necessarily in that order."

At first, we compared notes about our time in Europe. Where we went. What we did. Who we did it with. Webb had taken a trip to Sweden to check out the blondes. I had taken a trip to Italy to check out the brunettes. Both of us had gotten wasted during Oktoberfest in Munich.

"Christ," Spider laughed. "I probably dumped a schooner of beer on you. I was told I did that a lot, but I don't remember."

Finally, the conversation turned to Vietnam.

"So, you must have been there for Tet," I said.

I had already left Vietnam and was safely in Europe when the Viet Cong and North Vietnamese army launched a massive offensive on the Vietnamese New Year's Day in 1968. It turned out to be a huge military defeat for them, but Tet helped sharpen American public opinion against the war. The widespread attacks had occurred after our military leaders had said the enemy lacked the capacity to do what it had attempted to do.

Webb told me he'd had a close call.

"I was on my way to operations to work mids when a rocket came flying in," Spider recalled. "It bounced off the road in front of me, hurtled the chain-link fence and went off behind ops."

"Anybody get hurt?" I asked.

Spider shook his head. "Not that night."

"Not that night?"

Webb grew more serious. "We got hit again a few nights later, and a guy from B Company was killed."

B Company. My old outfit.

I leaned forward. "Anybody I know?"

After a brief pause, Spider asked: "Did you know Bill Cummings?"

It took me a few seconds to make the connection. "You mean, William Cummings?" A well-bred Virginian, Cummings, a traffic analyst like me, always insisted on being called by his given name, William. "He's dead?"

"A mortar round landed right on top of him while he was setting up a Claymore," Webb said. "It wasn't his job, but one of his bunkmates was on leave, and he was filling in for him. The mine went off, and he was vaporized."

While I was at Phu Bai, setting up a Claymore had been my job during alerts when all the soldiers at the field station took up positions in the trench line and bunkers along our compound's perimeter. At least a dozen times during my stay there I had crawled out beyond the trench line and slid the plastic-covered mine into a slot in a pre-placed concrete block. An electric magneto set off the device. We were warned not to attach its trigger, called "the Clacker" by those soldiers who used the weapon all the time, to the wire leads until we were a safe distance away from the Claymore.

When the mortar round hit, Cummings, obviously setting up one of the mines for the first time, must have been close to the fully armed Claymore. The sudden jolt must have activated the magneto. Everything went off at once, and he was gone.

"Did you know Bill?" Webb asked.

"Yeah, I knew William."

Cummings was one of the few guys I had met in Vietnam who really didn't have to be there. He had already finished a twelve-month tour. Before I arrived at Phu Bai, he had been reassigned to Vint Hill Farms, an ASA base near Warrenton, Virginia, not far from Fredericksburg, his hometown. Shortly after I arrived in Vietnam, Cummings returned.

No one knew why Cummings had volunteered to come back to the 8th RRFS. I had met other guys who had extended for another six months after serving one tour at Phu Bai, but he had decided to return after going back to the States for a few months.

"Maybe he likes the plastic eggs and reconstituted milk," one of my buddies suggested.

"Maybe it's the tax-free pay," another one chimed in.

Cummings didn't seem enamored of the work we did, mostly filling out long, detailed technical summaries about radio intercept. He always seemed to be in a sour mood. He complained a lot. A graduate of Virginia Commonwealth University, he was older than the rest of us. He was near the end of his four-year enlistment in the ASA. Like most of us, he had no intention of staying in the Army.

It took me awhile to learn why Cummings had returned to Phu Bai, but I figured it out.

Because of the highly classified nature of the work that went on at the 8th RRFS, Vietnamese workers and visitors had to be accompanied by an American soldier while on the post. They were not allowed to wander about. I was a Spec Four the entire time I was in Vietnam, and I caught escort duty every two months or so while I was there.

One time, I followed "The Ratman" around while he checked his traps. We didn't find any rodents. Judging from the size of the wire cages he used to catch them, the rats must have been huge. The Ratman, who was dressed in dingy shorts, a dirty t-shirt and a coolie hat, didn't speak any English, but he constantly flashed a rather cruel grin. It said, "I'm going to come back tonight and cut your balls off." I believed him.

Another time, I watched three Vietnamese men paint the interior of the day room, which served as a recreation area and a library. I had played a game of table tennis with one of them during their lunch break. He waxed me. Indigenous workers were supposed to be thoroughly vetted by the South Vietnamese government, but the guy I played ping-pong against turned out to be a Viet Cong agent. That afternoon, he was taken into custody as he left our post.

Several months after Cummings returned, I saw him walking with a pretty Vietnamese woman who worked in the RMK Construction office. It was the end of the work day, and I was leading a group of house girls who kept the officers' quarters clean to the main gate to catch the bus back to Hue.

I had spent one morning in the RMK office keeping an eye on the three young Vietnamese women who worked there while their bosses, two American civilians, were elsewhere. None of them gave me the impression they understood much English. They did smile a lot. The prettiest of them was now walking next to Cummings toward the main gate.

Cummings was a Spec Five, a noncommissioned officer. Because of his rank, he didn't have to pull escort duty. I wondered what he was doing with the woman. I only caught a fleeting glimpse of them, but it was enough for me to know Cummings wasn't escorting the pretty young woman anywhere. Instead, he was accompanying her on a leisurely stroll to the main gate. *A big difference.*

She wore a white *ao dai,* the traditional attire for young unmarried Vietnamese women. The work women I escorted wore faded tunics over their black pajama bottoms. All of them were probably married. While I walked behind the four house girls, making sure none of them got lost before we reached the main gate, Cummings hovered over his pretty companion. He walked as close as he could to her without touching her. He held his soft-brimmed boonie hat balled up in one of his hands while he talked intently to her, gesturing with his other hand. Apparently, he said something the girl liked. She smiled as they slowly walked along. During our five-minute walk, I didn't say a word to the women I accompanied. None of them smiled.

Cummings was then too wrapped up in his pretty companion to notice me. A few days later, as we sat alone working at our desks in our little corner in the operations center, I asked him about the girl.

"I met her the first time I was here, and I got to know her pretty well," he said. "I got to know her entire family. I often visited them at their home in Hue."

Cummings didn't say how he felt about the woman. He didn't have to. It was obvious. He cared enough about her to risk another twelve-month tour in Vietnam.

During Cummings' first Vietnam stint, Hue, a little more than twenty-five kilometers up Route One, had been open to the soldiers from the radio research station, but that had changed. Perhaps a week before I arrived, the old imperial capital was placed off-limits. Hue was deemed too dangerous. S2 didn't want a bunch of guys with top-secret crypto clearances running around loose.

From then on, the men assigned to the radio research unit spent most of their year in South Vietnam on the compound. We could go over to the airport across Route One and watch the planes land and take off, or we could walk out the back gate and trod the narrow path that had been cut through the minefield surrounding the post to visit the Marine commissary.

Most of the time, we stayed put.

Cummings didn't learn about the travel restriction until after he reported for duty at Phu Bai.

He had been dead nearly eighteen months when I ran into Spider at Fort Dix.

"Did anyone tell his girl?" I asked him.

"What girl?"

RADIO
DAYS

MARCH 1974

Normally, I made my run to Augusta from Portland on the first Saturday of every month. I'd leave the doors to my Toyota unlocked the night before outside my apartment in North Deering. The next morning, I'd find an old Army field jacket in the back seat with its pockets bulging with something. I never looked at the contents. I didn't want to know. All I knew was I was getting paid a hundred dollars to deliver whatever it was.

I was just getting by. I was going part-time to the University of Maine at Portland-Gorham, or Po-Go U as we students liked to call it, on the GI bill. To help make ends meet, I had cobbled together part-time gigs at two Portland AM radio stations. A couple of mornings a week I ran the board in the recording studio at one downtown station monitoring sound quality when the ad agencies cut their radio commercials. Saturday nights, I pulled a six-hour, on-air shift at another radio station.

Before my discharge from the Army, I passed the FCC's test for a third-class radiotelephone operator's license. While in South Vietnam, I had helped operate a station on the Military Amateur Radio System. MARS, which used a phone-patch telephone connection over a short-wave radio, was the only way most soldiers in Vietnam could call home. The license got me on the air.

Some of the DJs I knew used their real names. My radio handle was Rich Lotion. I got it off a bottle of hand cream. During my shift, I read the news and weather at the top of the hour, played the commercials as scheduled, and stuck to the playlist issued by the radio station's program director. "Play the music I tell you to play," he said. "No deviations." At most radio stations, the PD was the law. It wasn't my dream job, but it got my foot in the door.

A friend of my brother set me up with my once-a-month Saturday gig. At least my brother told me he was a friend.

"I want you to do a favor for a buddy of mine," he said, when he approached me with the idea. "There will be a couple of bucks in it for you." He didn't give me a name. He just said his friend would call me. And he did.

The hundred dollars was nearly enough to cover the monthly rent on my Ray Street place, a two-room apartment in an ell at the rear of a large colonial in the North Deering section of Portland. All I had to do was to drive my Toyota sixty miles up to Augusta once each month and drop off the field jacket at an apartment on Boothby Street. *Easy enough.*

After I had gotten out of the Army two years before, I bought a 1967 Corona from a friend of mine. He'd bought it for his wife, but she decided she didn't like to drive a standard shift. "She rode the clutch a lot," my friend confessed. His wife also had a knack for running into things. Nothing major, but the little white Corona was dinged up pretty bad. Small rust spots peppered its body. It looked like a clunker, but it ran pretty well.

Other than the money, I really didn't have a good reason to make the monthly run to Augusta, despite it being my hometown. While I was away in the Army, a lot of the people I had grown up with had finished college, gotten married or done both. It was like we were on two differ-ent planets. They had moved on, and I felt like I was just playing catch up.

More than likely, I never used whatever it was that I was transport-ing during my monthly trips to Augusta. I wasn't much into drugs. I had smoked a little pot and I tried speed one time, but that was it. My little sideline was my own form of protest, I guess. It was my chance to pull a fast one, to beat the system. A game I could play with the cops.

I was meticulous in my preparations. Before every run to Augusta, I went over a mental checklist. I tested the headlights — high and low beams. I made sure the directional signals worked. I topped off the gas tank and checked the oil and water levels.

I left little to chance. While on the road, I drove at or just under the speed limit. I didn't pass any vehicles, no matter how slow they were moving. I did nothing to draw attention to myself. I didn't want the police to stop me because of a traffic violation and somehow stumble across whatever I was carrying in the pocket of my field jacket.

Usually, everything went like clockwork. Then, one Saturday night I got a call while on the air at the radio station.

"We got something special for you." I recognized the deep resonant voice. "We'll pay you two bills, but you got to take it tonight."

Another shipment wasn't scheduled for two weeks. The call came during a commercial break. I had about a minute to talk before I had to go back on the air.

"Tonight?" I said. "I can't take it tonight. I got a date."

"Break it," the voice said. "We can't let this stuff sit. We got to move it."

After my shift ended, I was supposed to meet a blind date at Matty's in Westbrook. I'd already gotten lucky at that night spot a couple of times, but I guess my luck was about to run out. Blind dates didn't like to be stood up. I probably wouldn't get a second chance.

"Hold on a second," I said. "I got to push a button."

Slipping my headset back on, I listened as a 30-second ad about a sale at Porteous, Mitchell and Braun wound down. After glancing at the radio log, I cued up a cassette for a Pepsi ad. I pushed it in as the ad for the Portland department store ended. *Smooth.*

Then I got back to the phone call.

"Make it quick," I said. "I got 30 seconds."

The voice complied with my request.

"You driving the Toyota?"

"Yeah."

"Are the doors unlocked?"

I thought for a moment. "Yeah."

"Good," the voice said. "When you leave, the field jacket will be there."

Click. He hung up.

The radio station was located at the end of a dead-end dirt road in a field several hundred yards off Warren Avenue. A secluded spot. Not many people came down that road at night. If they did, I wouldn't know it. Like most broadcast booths, the one I worked in had no view of the outside world. DJs don't like distractions.

The Pepsi ad was due to end a few seconds after my caller rang off, so I cued up a record on one of the four turntables surrounding the console. As the 45 began to spin, I began the intro: "Hey," I said. "Here's a song for every guy who's ever been dumped. Smokey knows how it feels." Right on cue, Smokey Robinson's "Tracks of My Tears" began. *Tight.*

I had wanted to be a disc jockey ever since I watched Dan the Record Man broadcast his afternoon radio show from inside the storefront of the Nicholson and Ryan jewelry store in downtown Augusta during the 50s. A few afternoons after school, until I was shooed away, I hung around the WRDO studio, located on the second floor of a Water Street building.

Silently, I watched the DJs practicing their craft. Spinning records did involve some skill. On most 45s or LP album cuts, there was a slight delay before the music started after the stylus was placed on the first groove of vinyl. The trick was to fill that gap until the exact moment the music started. No more. No less. No dead air.

During my Saturday night gigs, I tried to perfect my timing as well as my on-air *persona*. Off the air, I was kind of shy and withdrawn. I tended to think a bit before I spoke. Behind the microphone I was different, a kind of wise guy. On the air, I had to think quick and talk fast but not sound like a babbling fool.

While hovering over the microphone, I focused my eyes on the wall behind it and conversed with someone I imagined was there. It was no one in particular. It could be a man or a woman. It didn't make any difference. For a few seconds, I'd devote my attention completely to that person.

As Smokey was about to stop singing, I cued up another record on another turntable. When the song ended, I waited one or two beats before beginning my patter. "Hey, we're still waiting for the ice to go out on Sebago," I whined, "and Terry Jacks is still singing about 'Seasons in the Sun.' " *Boom.* The music began.

And so it went until the station sign-off at midnight. Then, after flicking off the lights and locking the door behind me, I hustled out to my car. The field jacket was in the back seat. After bringing it up front with me, I could feel the bulges in both front pockets. They were larger than usual. I was curious. For the first time I had to know what I was carrying.

After taking a good look around to make sure I was alone, I flicked on the dome light. Reaching into one of the pockets, I pulled out a small package wrapped in brown paper. The folds in the paper came undone as I held it in the palm of my hand. Like a blooming plant, the paper unfolded to reveal two thin brown bricks of hashish, each measuring about five inches wide and seven inches long. The marijuana was thoroughly compressed and the little bricks were heavier than they looked. I hefted one. It weighed about a pound.

After carefully rewrapping the package, I slid the hash back into its hiding place. Then I reached into the other pocket of the field jacket and removed the other package. Two more bricks of hash. Same size. Same weight.

I had gotten wrecked both times I'd tried hash. Once, it was with a group of teeny boppers in a cabin up in Vassalboro. It was a free ride. Another time I was with an old Army buddy in Connecticut. We split a gram. We paid five dollars for it. Then we drove around New London taking hits off a water pipe. Both times, it seemed everything moved in slow motion. *Too slow.* Hashish was way too much of a high for me.

I figured I was carrying about two kilos of hash. I did the math. It was worth about ten thousand dollars on the street. I shuddered to think what would happen if I got caught with it. I had been better off not knowing what had been jammed into the front pockets of the field jacket. Now I had something to worry about. I'd have to be especially careful on my drive north to Augusta.

All went well until I left Interstate 295. I took the last exit north in Brunswick and drove through the darkened downtown across the Androscoggin River into Topsham before I ran into trouble. As I headed up Route 201 toward Bowdoinham, I heard a ping from behind the floorboard in front of the pedals. It was like something had let go. When I depressed the clutch to shift into fourth gear, the pedal went all the way to the floor with absolutely no resistance. I had no clutch, and the engine whined as the car remained in third gear.

I didn't panic. *Not yet.* In the past, I had often shifted into fourth gear or downshifted into second or third gear without even using the clutch. Usually, I could feel the shifting points in the Toyota's four-speed synchromesh transmission. For that split second, I could move the stick smoothly into the next gear without any problems. No grinding.

As long as nobody suddenly stopped right in front of me, I knew I could go through the gears, up or down, without much difficulty. I kept driving north. At this time of night, there wasn't much traffic, and I was able to drive the next twenty miles or so without a hitch alternating between third and fourth gear. I drove slowly.

While coasting down the steep hill from the Commons in Gardiner, I managed to downshift gradually by pumping the brake to slow the car. By the time I reached Water Street and slowly rolled through the yellow flashing light, I was back in first gear. No problem.

After driving through the intersection, I worked my way up to third gear while I continued north up 201 toward Augusta. A couple of miles later in Farmingdale I pulled up behind a slow-moving car. Suddenly, without warning, it came to a dead stop. Then the driver flicked on his directional to turn left, and the car quickly shot across Maine Avenue and headed up into Hayford Heights.

To avoid slamming into the back of the car, I had to hit the brakes and bring the Toyota to nearly a complete stop while in third gear. The car jerked as the engine began to stall. Before it died, I managed to pull the car off the road in front of a florist shop.

The Toyota was stuck in third gear. It was after one o'clock in the morning, and I wasn't driving any farther that night with that car.

As I sat in the car wondering how I was going to deliver the hash, a set of bright red taillights pulled off the road and came to a stop right in front of me. In my headlights, I could see the rear end of a pick-up truck with the letters F O R D running across the tailgate. A few seconds later, I saw the large dark outline of someone walking toward my car just outside the beam of light. As the figure approached the driver's side of the car, I could make out who it was. A cop!

My heart began hammering against my chest when the policeman reached the driver's side door. I quickly rolled down the window.

"What's seems to be the problem here?" the cop asked, leaning down toward me.

"Did, did I do something wrong?" I stammered, stealing a quick glance toward the field jacket, which lay neatly folded next to me in the passenger seat.

"No, I don't think you did anything wrong," the cop chuckled. "If you did, I couldn't do anything about it. I'm a little bit out of my jurisdiction." He turned his body so I could see the Gardiner Police Department shoulder patch. "Anyway, I'm off duty, and just stopped to see if you needed any help."

When he had turned and leaned in to show me his shoulder patch, his unbuttoned jacket opened and I caught sight of the badge and the nametag on his blue blouse. His name was Larrabee.

I had had a little experience in dealing with the police. Twice, I had gotten picked up for traffic violations, both a long time before I began hauling marijuana. Once, I got ticketed for going through a red light down in Randolph. I was paying too much attention to the inside of the thigh of the girl I was with and not enough attention to where I was going. Another time, a state cop wrote me up for doing fifty in a thirty-five mile per-hour zone. He stopped me on State Street not far from the

State House dome. I didn't have a girl with me that time, but I could have been thinking about one.

When it came to the police, I knew to keep my mouth shut. I let them take the lead in the conversation. No lively patter. No wise cracks. Definitely no attitude. *Just the facts, ma'am.*

This situation was different. This cop was here to help me, not to write me up. At least that was what he said. That didn't make me breathe any easier.

"So what happened?"

"I think I lost my clutch," I said. "See?" I pressed the clutch all the way to the floor and fiddled with the stick shift. Nothing happened. "It's stuck."

"I can see that." Larrabee rubbed the side of his face as if he was trying to find a solution to my problem.

"You got Triple A?" he asked.

I shook my head. "No."

"You got anybody you can call?"

"Not at this time of night."

Larrabee thought some more.

"Well, where ya going, anyway?"

As much as possible, I tried to stick to the truth.

"I'm going up to Augusta to see a friend," I answered. That was close to the truth.

"Ohhh," responded Larrabee.

"He doesn't have a car," I quickly added. "Doesn't even have a telephone." I didn't know whether my *friend* did have a car or a telephone, but adhering strictly to the truth might create problems for me. A little lie might not hurt.

"Where does your friend live?"

"In Royal Park," I answered.

"Where's that?" asked Larrabee.

"Down over the hill at the end of State Street."

Larrabee grunted. He'd come to a conclusion.

"Look, why don't you grab your things and lock up your car," he instructed. "I'll give you a ride to where you've got to go. I'm headed to Augusta to see my girlfriend." Then he tugged at the left sleeve of his jacket and glanced at his watch. "That is, if she's still up."

When Larrabee stepped away from the car, I climbed out and started to put the key in the door. I wasn't sure if accepting a ride from a cop was the right thing to do, but I knew I didn't want to be stranded in Farmingdale with two kilos of hash in my car. Maybe the next cop who happened along would be more curious. I started to walk toward Larrabee's truck.

"Hey," he called out. "Don't forget your jacket. It's supposed to get cold again tomorrow."

The field jacket. Right, I must not forget the field jacket. That might put me in a world of hurt. I didn't even know if it fit me, but Larrabee was correct. I shouldn't leave it behind.

Simultaneously, we climbed into the cab of Larrabee's F100. While he got comfortable behind the steering wheel, I arranged myself on the passenger side of the cab with the field jacket neatly folded on my lap.

I was nervous as hell.

I sniffed the air.

"Sorry about the smell," Larrabee apologized. "I haven't cleaned my truck in a while. Drives my girlfriend crazy."

When I sniffed I wasn't concerned about how bad Larrabee's truck smelled. I was checking to see if the hashish gave out any telltale odor. It didn't.

"You're lucky," Larrabee said, as he slowly pulled his pickup back onto Maine Avenue and headed north.

"I am?" I really didn't know what he meant.

"Yeah," he said. "Usually my shift ends at midnight, but I worked some OT tonight. Had to clear an accident on 24 down in South Gardiner. Guy hit a tree while trying to avoid a deer. He was drunker than a skunk. I had a lot of paperwork to do."

I didn't feel lucky. I felt like I was walking a tightrope without a safety net.

Larrabee went on: "He didn't kill the deer, though. I had to track it down to put it out of its misery. It was a doe. Then, a couple of state troopers came along and took the carcass. They said they would give it to some poor people, but I think it's going to end up in one of their freezers. What do you think?"

My mind was definitely on something else, and I didn't know what to say, but I felt I should give Larrabee an answer. "You might be right," was the best I could come up with it.

As we coasted down the steep hill entering Hallowell, Larrabee took his right hand off the steering wheel and pointed to the field jacket. For a second, I thought he was going to touch it and I contemplated jumping out of the truck.

"So you were in the Army, huh?"

"Yeah," I said. "I was in the Army." At least I was back to telling the truth. That felt a little bit better.

"Were you in Nam?"

"Yeah," I nodded. "I was in Vietnam for a while."

Larrabee told me he was drafted into the Army in 1956, long before Vietnam became a hot spot.

"I fought the Battle of Fort Dix," he said. "I was a clerk in one of the training companies."

I told him I had gone through basic training and advanced individual training at the New Jersey army base after I was drafted in 1970. I spent nearly five months there before shipping out.

"Nam was a pretty rough place, huh?" Larrabee was probing, but I could tell he didn't know how deep he could go.

"It had its moments," I said. I looked out the window as we cruised past all the closed antique shops in downtown Hallowell.

"I don't mean to make you feel uncomfortable," Larrabee apologized again. "I know a lot of you guys from Nam don't like to talk about it."

Officer Larrabee was right. I did feel uncomfortable, but not for the reason he thought. Under different circumstances, I would have told him what life was like for me while serving with a transportation outfit on Vinh Loc Island, a supply hub near the mouth of the Perfume River in Vietnam's northernmost I Corps. But not tonight.

We drove past an Augusta police car parked in front of the Dairy Queen near the Augusta-Hallowell line. The driver of the cruiser flashed his lights as Larrabee's truck rolled past.

"A friend of mine," Larrabee explained. "He's caught the graveyard shift this weekend."

I hoped Larrabee's "friend" didn't pull out and follow us, but I didn't look back to check. I kept my eyes on the street ahead and my mouth shut.

After we threaded our way through the empty west-side rotaries, I grew more nervous as Larrabee drove farther down State Street toward the Kennebec County Jail, but he didn't stop and I breathed a little easier.

A minute later, as we headed down Gaslight Hill toward Mount Vernon Avenue, I said: "It's the left at the bottom of the hill."

Larrabee grunted.

It had taken us about ten minutes to cover the five miles from where Larrabee had picked me up. He let me off in front of a little mom-and-pop grocery store on Boothby Street.

"My friend lives upstairs in the back," I said, pointing to the second floor of the building after I got out of his truck. "Thanks for the lift."

Moving as quietly as I could, I hustled up the stairs and walked into the shadows toward the rear of the second-floor porch. There I stood with my heart still racing and waited.

Turning around at the end of the dead-end street, Larrabee headed back toward its intersection with State Street. After he made the turn, I moved forward so I could view the entire length of Boothby Street, streetlight to streetlight. It took another five minutes for me to calm down.

When I was sure Larrabee was gone for good, I flew down the stairs and headed toward a small house on the other side of the street. I walked up the driveway and opened the storm door at its rear entrance.

Normally, I hung the jacket on a little hook on the back door and took the envelope taped to the window in the door. Usually, it contained five crisp twenty-dollar bills.

This time, when I tried to hang up the coat, the door opened slightly.

"Come on in," I heard someone say from inside the darkened room. "Close the door behind you and don't move."

My first instinct was to run, but I didn't think I would be able to get that far. I did as I was told.

"Where's the Toyota?" the voice asked me.

As my eyes slowly adjusted to the darkness, I could make out the outline of a refrigerator on the left side of the room and the dark form of large man leaning back against the counter on the far side of the kitchen.

He spoke just above a whisper, but his voice resonated quite well in the small room. It was what would be considered a "ballsy voice" for radio, low and deep. It sounded familiar. It was the same man who called me at the radio station.

I told him about the clutch.

The shadowy figure on the other side of the room took some time to digest this information. After a few moments of consideration, he asked another question.

"Who brought you here?"

I told him how an off-duty Gardiner policeman had stopped to help me.

Again my answer was followed by a period of silence. I didn't dare say a word, but I did wonder what was going to happen next.

"You let a cop bring you here?" The voice sounded incredulous.

"Well, not exactly here," I answered. I explained how I had Larrabee drop me off at the tenement on the other side of the street and how I had waited five minutes after he left before coming to my real destination.

Apparently, the voice had witnessed the arrival and the departure of Larrabee's pickup.

"I wondered what was going on," he intoned.

"He offered to give me a ride," I explained. "If I turned it down, I thought it would look suspicious."

"What was his name?"

I told him.

"Larrabee?" he laughed. "Shit, that guy couldn't find a nut if you gave him a can of cashews."

I didn't join in his laughter.

Instead, I held the field jacket up in front of me. "I made sure to bring this along. I didn't want to leave this behind."

"Put the jacket on the table," the voice ordered. "It's right there in front of you."

Suddenly, I heard a metallic click. I wasn't sure what it was, but I braced myself for what might come next. Then, I heard another click followed by a little flash of light and an intake of breath as the man on the other side of the kitchen took a first deep drag on a cigarette.

I took a step forward and placed the jacket on the table. I quickly backed away. I didn't want to get any closer to the voice than I already was.

"What are you going to do about the car?"

That was a good question. I didn't have a good answer.

"I don't know," I didn't know, really, but I thought it was best if I came up with some sort of answer.

"My brother might know somebody with a tow bar," I said. "First, I'll have to get the car out of there. Then, I'll have to find someone who can fix it. I hope it's just the clutch and not the whole transmission."

That was followed by a period of silence. *Dead air.* I didn't dare try to fill this gap. No pithy remarks. No attitude. I just stood there. I hoped the man would simply ask another question. I prayed he wouldn't do anything else.

I could hear the ticking of the clock on the wall next to the door behind him. The seconds passed excruciatingly slow.

Abruptly, the voice stated: "You can leave now."

I quickly turned to walk out the door.

"Don't forget to take your envelope," he called out after me.

I left the envelope where it was. I didn't want to play this game anymore.

"I don't want it," I said. I had one foot out the door when I added: "You can keep the jacket, too. I don't think I'm cut out for this kind of work."

As I closed the door behind me, I thought I heard the voice say something, but I wasn't sure. Maybe, he was just clearing his throat. I just kept walking.

Final Respects

———◆———

JANUARY **1991**

The old man sat alone in the last row of chairs set up for visitors at the funeral home. Everyone else who came to pay respects spent a few moments looking at my mother in the open casket. Most of them remarked how good she looked.

Murphy, the mortician, had worked his magic. On her cheeks, "Murph The Turf," as I called him, had replaced the drab pallor of her final days with a healthy-looking roseate. When she was alive, my mother had seldom worn makeup, so the face on the body inside the coffin bore only a faint resemblance. She had been placed inside of her best dress and a peaceful expression was fixed on her face. Her folded hands held a prayer card and entwined rosary.

My brother was the first to notice the old man.

"Who's he?" he whispered.

We stood off to one side in front of the long, narrow room, close to the floral arrangements surrounding the casket. One of Murphy's assistants had handed me a clipboard. On it was the list of the drivers of the cars in the next day's funeral procession. I had been trying to figure out who would be assigned to which car when my brother posed his question.

I looked up, asking "Who's who?" as I followed his gaze. I expected to see some obscure cousin, a member of our large extended family seldom seen in between funerals and weddings. But I was surprised. The old man was a complete stranger. I had no idea who he was, nor why he was spending the better part of a rare sunny Tuesday afternoon in January at a funeral parlor. For a time, I had stood at the door greeting visitors, accepting their condolences. I didn't recall seeing the old man come in. He must have slipped past me.

For a few moments, we watched him. The old man never approached the casket. He sat alone, he spoke to no one, and no one said a word to him.

"Where's Dad?" I asked. Big Jim might know who the stranger was. He knew all sorts of people, for all sorts of reasons. Maybe the man was an old friend of his. A former business associate. A drinking buddy. Someone he owed money.

"He's downstairs," my brother said. The funeral home was a rabbit warren of little rooms, with lots of places for my father to hide. "He's taking a nap."

Our father had the uncanny ability to catch a few winks, anytime, anywhere. It didn't matter. He was always able to nod off. A catnap. Ten, fifteen minutes. Then he'd wake up. "Just like new," he would offer.

"Sleeps like a rock," I said admiringly. It was a trait I didn't inherit.

"That he can sleep without any guilt is the amazing thing," my brother observed.

"He has no conscience," I said, "asleep or awake."

To us, Big Jim had a lot to feel guilty about, but if he knew it, he never let on. He just rolled merrily along. Life was a joke. Everyday was a party.

Even his nickname was funny. To start with, our father was not a big man. He stood barely five feet tall. When he was young, his friends apparently sensed he intended to live large, so they put "Big" in front of his difficult-to pronounce French first name, which they changed to "Jim." Thus, Big Jim was born. He liked it.

My mother also received a nickname. But hers was a burden. Christened Matilde, an old family name, she'd been called "Tilly" for most of her life. She hated both her given name and the moniker her siblings had hung on her. "Silly Tilly," her brothers and sisters called her. She put up with it.

My mother put up with a lot of things. It was her style and a survival skill she had honed to perfection. Lord knows, she had a lot of practice. Life with Big Jim would challenge a saint. My mother was no candidate for canonization, but she tried to be a good Catholic woman, working hard to earn her place in heaven. At the very least, she had the patience of a saint, a virtue continually tested during her forty-five years of marriage to Big Jim.

Our mother died from complications following a stroke. But my brother and I were convinced she had just run out of patience. Finally. On the morning she had her seizure, she was waiting at home for our father. They were supposed to go shopping. After she suffered her stroke, she lay helpless on the floor in the bedroom for most of the day before he showed up.

Of course, it wasn't Big Jim's fault. He had no way of knowing his wife was about to have a stroke. But my brother and I had always thought it would have been nice if he had stuck around the house a little bit more to keep an eye on his wife. Our mother had been on a downward slide for a long time. If our father had noticed, it didn't register. After all, to Big Jim, life was just a party. Don't worry. Be happy.

Now, we were gathered at the funeral home to pay our last respects, and this stranger didn't fit in with the other visitors. While my aunts and uncles huddled in the front of the room, babbling away in the French patois spoken in our part of Maine, and my cousins, several of Tilly's countless nieces and nephews, gravitated toward the back of the room, as far away from her casket as possible, the old man continued to sit in the middle tier of folding chairs all by himself.

Apparently, nobody knew who he was.

My brother broke the ice. "Excuse me, sir," he said, sitting down next to him. "Did you know my mother?" I took a seat on the other side of the visitor.

The old man shook his head. Up close, we could see he was much older than our mother had been when she died, maybe in his early eighties. He hadn't shaved that morning, and the day-old stubble matched the color of his hair, enhancing the overall grimness of his countenance.

The old man didn't smile. He didn't frown. His expression remained neutral. It was as if he was on some sort of drug; something to help him avoid the peaks and valleys and keep everything level.

"I knew her only when she was a young woman," he said, looking toward her casket. His speech was deliberate, barely audible. My brother and I leaned forward to listen. "She was young and vibrant, so full of life." His voice was tinged with sadness.

My brother started to make introductions. It wasn't necessary. He knew who we were.

"You were the soldier," he said, interrupting my brother and turning toward me. "You went to Vietnam." Then, to my brother, after slowly swiveling in his seat, "And you stayed home."

The Vietnam War had always been a sore subject between us. I went. He didn't. To avoid the draft, my brother didn't run off to Canada. But he did make himself scarce. Then, when the draft lottery started, he got lucky. His birth date drew a high number. Vietnam was something we never discussed; a raw nerve we just didn't touch.

The old man wasn't done. He looked toward the front of the room, where our younger sister sat talking with two of our aunts. "And she," he pointed, "she is the one with all of the husbands."

Not exactly. True, our sister had been married twice. But the rest of the men in her life had been just a steady parade of live-ins. "Disposable men," she called them like Bic Lighters or ball-point pens. At the moment, my sister had no significant other, nor, for that matter, an insignificant other. But she was always looking.

My brother, who was a little younger than me, also had been married twice. After his second divorce, which featured a nasty legal battle for the custody of his two kids, he'd given up. "All I want now is a meaningless relationship," he had told me. "It doesn't have to last beyond a weekend."

Unlike my siblings, I had managed to remain married for twenty years. After a rocky start, my wife and I had grown comfortable with each other. We had a solid marriage. A good relationship. The family curse had passed me by.

It was clear the old man knew who we were. But we had no idea who he was and still no clue why he had come to pay his final respects to our mother.

"So you knew our my mother when she young?" It was my question.

The old man thought for a moment, accentuating the deep furrows on his forehead. "Well, we never really spoke to each other," he admitted. "Back then, I'd see her a lot. On the street."

The old man told us he lived on Summer Street, off the upper end of Bridge Street on Augusta's west side, right around the corner from the funeral home.

Sometime before World War II, my grandfather put up three apartment houses on the steep part of Bridge Street between State and Water. The triple deckers were built right into the side of a hill. In two of the buildings, two of my uncles had opened businesses, a bar and a small grocery store, at street level on the ground floor. For a time, most of the flats were occupied by aunts and uncles.

Right up until she got married, in her late twenties, my mother lived with her parents in one of the apartments. In those days, single women stayed home with their families. Before they wed, few of them ventured far outside the nest.

Back then, my mother worked in one of the department stores, "Five and Dimes," as she called them, down on Water Street, a short walk down the hill from the triple deckers. Several times each day she made the trip. Down and Up. Lunch. Supper. Then home to bed.

Everyone walked everywhere then. From where he lived, the old man would have taken the same route downtown as Tilly. There would have been lots of chances for them to see each other.

"You might say we had a nodding acquaintance," he explained.

When we were young, our parents had told us how they had met one day during the war when my mother was walking up Bridge Street.

Our father spent the early years of World War II in Maine as a crewman on the shore batteries in the Harpswells and Cape Elizabeth. "I fought in the Battle of Casco Bay," he'd laugh. For months on end, he'd hitchhike home to Augusta on weekends. "Christ," he said. "Half the town thought I was AWOL." Following D-Day, my father was assigned to an artillery outfit in France, where he loaded shells into a 105-millimeter howitzer. He had arrived in time to participate in the push into Belgium and fight in the Battle of the Bulge.

It was while he was on one of those weekends home, not long before he shipped out to Europe, that he ran into Tilly.

Years before, their families had lived side-by-side on Bond Street, a street filled with short, squat tenements near the base of Sand Hill in Augusta's French-Canadian north end. However, they had never met until the day he followed Tilly up Bridge Street to her house. Apparently, Big Jim liked the way she walked.

My father knew one of Tilly's older brothers, who was with the Army fighting in the South Pacific. He stopped in to see her parents and check on how her brother was doing. It turned into a long visit. He stayed for supper.

After that, until he went overseas, Big Jim spent most of his weekend passes with Tilly. After he shipped out, they wrote each other. Love blossomed.

Following his discharge from the Army, they married.

I wondered if the old man knew any of this. "Do you know my father?" I asked.

"Never met him," came the terse response, "but I know of him."

A lot of people in Augusta knew of Big Jim. In a town renowned for its sameness, where everyone seemed to try to fit it, he stood out. He was rather flamboyant, a real character. No matter what, Big Jim always wore a suit and tie. Even when it became fashionable to dress casually, he continued to dress up. "If you want to do good, you have to look good," he'd say. It was his trademark.

Big Jim considered himself a natural-born salesman. "I got the gift of gab," he'd tell us. He sold everything. At least once. Life Insurance. Real Estate. Cars and trucks. Radio spots. Aluminum siding. For a time, he even went door-to-door peddling encyclopedias. Always, in a suit and tie. His attire didn't help.

Evidently, Big Jim did a lot more talking than selling. Closing a sale was not a strength of his. Sooner or later, this shortcoming became apparent to his employers. Eventually, each one of them had to let him go, albeit reluctantly. After all, it was pleasant to have my father around. "We hate to do this," they'd invariably say, "but sales are down, and we have to let you go." My father spent a lifetime drifting from one sales job to another, looking for just the right fit to match his talents. He never found it.

If it bothered him, Big Jim never let on. For a long time, that was the main problem in his marriage. If anything bothered Big Jim, he never let on. It drove my mother crazy. That wasn't all. If something was wrong, Big Jim didn't want to hear about it. "I got enough problems," he'd tell my mother. "I don't need any more." My parents talked, but they didn't talk much.

That was the atmosphere in which we grew up. Apparently, it was contagious. Nobody said anything to anybody. Not really. After we grew up, all of us had similar problems with meaningful communication. My brother and sister paid dearly for their inability, or unwillingness, to talk. Failed marriages. Ruined relationships.

I had been lucky. I had married a woman who was more understanding. She straightened me right out. "You better start talking to me, buster, or I'm out of here," she told me when we first wed. I learned to open up. Or else.

The old man at the funeral home had never married. "Guess I never found anybody who would have me," he explained. For an instant, his thin lips broke into a little smile, before settling back into his characteristic neutral expression. "When it came to women, I was kind of shy."

For most of his life, the old man had worked in the "shoe shops," moving from one little factory to another in Augusta, Hallowell or Gardiner.

"Use to take the bus to Gardiner to work," he told us. That bus didn't run anymore. "Use to do piece work," he explained. "The more shoes I made the more money I got." Most factory workers now were paid an hourly wage. It was the law.

The old man showed us his hands. His fingers were bent into permanent curls. "Arthur-itis," he said, mispronouncing his condition. He tried to splay them without success. I suspected it was Carpal Tunnel Syndrome and told him so. "Hurts like hell, and I can never straighten them out."

Even before the shoe factories began to close, the old man had moved on. He went to work for a cobbler down on Water Street, replacing soles and heels and buffing worn leather. But business became slow. "Nowadays, people just throw their old shoes away," he said. "They go out and buy another pair. They don't get their shoes repaired." When the shop closed, the old man retired. He began drawing Social Security.

The old man told us he lived in a small apartment in the house his parents had left him on Summer Street. He leased out the rest of the building. It was the same place he lived when he used to see Tilly walking up and down Bridge Street. "It was just like yesterday," he said, somewhat wistfully. "I can still see her walking up that hill."

All in all, the old man described a pretty depressing existence to us. In some ways, life hadn't been much better for our mother. For a long time in their marriage, our parents went on as before. Big Jim tried to sell. Tilly stayed at home. Neither was happy. Neither was sad. They just were.

My father also had a problem none of us kids knew about until we grew up. Big Jim had difficulty keeping his pants zipped. Our old man was a philanderer.

Apparently, his gift of gab was good for something. He couldn't sell a fig, but he knew how to close the deal when it came to women. It was one sale he could make.

I didn't learn about this until I came home from Vietnam.

Early one morning, while on leave, I returned from a night out to find my mother asleep on the couch in the living room. I woke her up.

"What's the matter?" I asked. Even in the dim light I could see she'd been crying.

"It's your father," she said. "He didn't come home."

"Where is he?"

The crying began again. "I don't know," she sobbed.

I tried to talk to my mother about it. But she clammed up. Rolling into a tight ball on the couch, she didn't say another word. As I fired off a litany of questions, all I heard were her quiet little sniffles.

"How long has this been going on? Who is he with? What does he tell you when he comes home?" One after another my queries came, but my mother didn't answer any of them. Then, I ended with the most important question of all: "What are you going to do about it?"

Still no answer. Then came my unsolicited advice.

"I know what I would do," I said. "I'd throw him out. Get rid of him. You don't need him."

My mother had no reaction. None I could discern anyway. I knew she wouldn't do anything. Everything would remain the same. Nothing would change. Tilly would spend the rest of her life waiting for Big Jim to come home.

One morning a few years later, when I was going to the University of Maine, my mother called me at my apartment in Old Town. She was looking for my father.

"He was supposed to come back from a sales trip up to The County yesterday, but he never did," she explained. "I thought he might have stopped to see you."

"No, Mom," I said. "I haven't seen him." Unless accompanied by Tilly, Big Jim never visited me while I was at college. "I'm sorry, but I can't help you." It was the end of the conversation. We exchanged good-byes. My mother hung up. She went back to waiting.

The day after my mother died, I visited one of my aunts, a sister-in-law she had been especially close to. She told me a doctor had recommended surgery to clear a blockage in my mother's Carotid Artery. She declined. My aunt said my mother never told my father about this. I think I know why.

As I sat next to the old man, I realized he had spent his whole life waiting for something that was never going to happen. It was obvious he'd carried a torch for my mother. Finally, it was time to put it out.

"We appreciate your coming," I told him. "It was nice to meet you." When my brother and I moved away, the old man got up to leave.

A few moments later, after we had returned to our station near the front of the room, Big Jim strode in.

"Who's the old fart?" he asked, catching sight of the old man shuffling toward the door at the other end of the room. No one else heard his comment over the din of conversation.

"An old friend of Mom's," I answered.

Big Jim squinted as he studied the slow-moving man.

"Doesn't look like anybody I know," he said, moving off to take a seat next to our sister.

"He never liked any of Mom's friends, anyway," my brother said.

We watched the old man slowly move through the door.

"Back when they were both walking up Bridge Street, what if that old man had said something to Mom?" my brother asked.

I looked to where our father sat.

"Things might have been different," I said.

Yeah," said my brother, following my gaze. "Real different."

"One thing for sure," I said, putting an arm around his shoulders. "We wouldn't be having this conversation."

New China Hotel

April 2002

I was in Hong Kong on a working vacation when I got a call from Sol, an assignment editor at a news magazine I had freelanced for in the past. I was in between books, so when I received the offer to write an article about how the residents of the former British crown colony were faring after five years under the rule of the People's Republic of China, I jumped at it. Perhaps a different kind of writing challenge would help end the malaise that had settled upon me following the release of my last thriller four years before. I didn't need the money, but my agent had been chiding me to get my ass in gear. Apparently, he was feeling the financial pinch.

When the Brits ceded control of the crown colony in 1997, Hong Kong became a special administrative region of the People's Republic. For the five-year anniversary of that event, the magazine wanted me to write an article focused on how the change had affected the people who lived there. Ultimately, the little people pay the highest price when change occurs. The magazine wanted me to write about them.

After agreeing to write the story, I enlisted the services of an interpreter, Peter Lee. Most of the people I wanted to talk to only spoke a smattering of English, and Mr. Lee was facile in both Cantonese and Mandarin. Through him, I interviewed street vendors, a schoolteacher, a cab driver, a couple of cooks, a stock analyst, a nightclub hostess and a dockworker.

Basically, all of them sang the same song. "Everything's fine. Nothing has changed." However, none of them wanted me to use their real names in the article. Folks in Hong Kong always have tried to hedge their bets.

It took parts of three days for me to collect enough information to write the magazine piece. Starting in my newspaper days, I've always worked like a squirrel, gathering as many nuts as I could before I sat down to write. I had enough material to do a decent three-thousand-word piece or about three-and-a half pages of magazine type. Add photos and captions, and I thought I had the makings of a good spread.

I had nearly completed the article when I got another call from Sol. He wondered whether I could hop up to Taipei for a few days to work on a second piece. He said the magazine would pick up the tab. Apparently, I had become the publication's Far East correspondent.

During an earthquake the week before, two construction cranes had toppled from the 56th floor of Taipei 101, a 1,669-foot office tower under construction in Taiwan's capital. The accident killed five construction workers. Apparently, it also renewed concerns about the viability of such a project in the middle of a city prone to tremors and monsoon winds. Pending the outcome of an investigation, work was halted on the building, projected to become the tallest man-made structure in the world.

"Just do what you do," Sol said. "Find out how people feel about these tall buildings falling down on them. We think it would make a terrific sidebar to the main bar you're working on. You know, the new Hong Kong versus the new Taipei. That sort of thing."

I gladly accepted the new assignment, and I asked Peter Lee if he could accompany me to Taiwan.

"I am sorry," he said, "but I can't go to Taipei."

"Why not?"

"Political reasons." Mr. Lee didn't explain further. I didn't pry. It was none of my business. Perhaps it was better if I didn't know.

"But I know someone who might be able to help you," he volunteered.

I was intrigued.

Mr. Lee went on to tell me about Julie Chen.

"In Taipei, she does what I do for visitors here in Hong Kong."

A slim Chinese man in his early sixties, Peter Lee was not prone to smile much, but he seemed to lighten up as he talked about Miss Chen.

"For a woman of her origins, she has carved out a niche for herself in a society where blood lines count," he said. "We Chinese are quite class conscious, you know. The Cantonese term for her would be *chop chung kwai*, mixed race devil, but she hasn't let that slow her down."

A hint of a smile played at Mr. Lee's lips.

"She is very good at what she does, but it is strictly business," he said, wagging a finger at me. "No hanky panky."

There was no formal arrangement, but they did send customers to each other occasionally, Mr. Lee said. "If you would like, I could see if she is available and arrange for her to serve as your guide in Taipei," he said.

"I would like that very much," I nodded. "I'm really looking forward to going to Taipei, and it will be good to have a guide who knows what she is doing."

I didn't tell Mr. Lee why I was so enthusiastic about my new assignment. It didn't have anything to do with Julie Chen. I didn't tell him that I had been to Taipei before, and I was eager to return.

October 1966

My first trip to Taipei came quite by accident. I was an Army supply clerk stationed with a MACV unit up in I Corps during the Vietnam War. After seven months in-country, I received orders to spend five days of R&R in Kuala Lumpur, Malaysia. I had never heard of the place.

As I walked into the small Marine air terminal in Da Nang, a group of men filed out the door at the front of the room.

"Where are they going?" I asked the lance corporal who stood at the lectern at the head of several rows of empty wooden benches.

"Taipei," he answered as he organized the sheaf of papers on his clipboard.

I looked at my travel orders.

"How long does it take to fly to Kuala Lumpur?" I asked.

"About four hours," the clerk answered.

"How long does it take to fly to Taipei?"

"Four, five hours."

The real difference was that the flight to Taipei was leaving immediately. The flight to Malaysia wasn't scheduled to leave for another two hours or so.

"Sure wish I was going to Taipei," I lamented, primarily to myself.

Barely a second went by before the lance corporal reached for the copy of the orders I held in my hand. A quick flourish of his pen, and the change was made.

"You now have orders to travel to Taipei, Taiwan," he announced. "You better run to catch the plane."

April 2002

Peter Lee may not have been welcomed in Taiwan, but he still had some pull. He was able to get me a seat on a Dragonair freighter carrying a load of computer components to Songshan International Airport.

Miss Chen met me at the airport.

She appeared to be a perfect blend of East and West. Her hair, worn in a stylish cut just off her shoulders, was dark with just a hint of natural curl. Her eyes were slightly slanted, but their hazel hue betrayed her western origins. Her skin color was lighter than the other Asian women I'd seen. Her nose was small, but it was straight and slightly upturned.

Julie Chen was pretty, but I had no prurient interest in her. In my mid-fifties, with my mid-life crises behind me, I hoped, I was less interested in sex and more interested in simply getting to know people, and, more importantly, getting along with them. Besides, as Peter Lee predicted, Miss Chen was all business.

During the drive in her Nissan sedan into the city's center, where Mr. Lee had booked my stay at the Imperial Hotel, she filled me in on what she knew about the accident at Taipei 101.

"Apparently, the two cranes that fell had been used in a construction project elsewhere and were recently installed on the 56th floor," she reported. "Four other cranes, which were designed and installed specifically for this project, were undamaged."

"How do you know this?" I asked.

"I sometimes work as a guide for some American engineers who are involved in the project," she said. "They told me why the building survived the earthquake. They think construction will resume soon."

Miss Chen went on to describe the safety features that were supposed to keep the skyscraper stable during high monsoon winds and earthquakes. She told me that the architectural plans called for the installation of a tuned mass damper in its upper reaches. The swaying pendulum was supposed to offset movements of the building in gusts of up to 137 miles per hour. The foundation was reinforced by 308 piles driven 80 meters into the ground, extending 30 meters into bedrock. "That was one of the reasons the entire building didn't topple during the earthquake," Miss Chen explained. "It is anchored solidly to the ground."

Taipei 101's builders employed the use of the five elements of *feng shui*, an ancient Chinese superstition, to bring the huge structure into harmony with its surroundings. From what Miss Chen told me, its designers went to great lengths to make sure the building would always be surrounded by good *karma*.

"The number 4 is considered unlucky by the Chinese," she explained. "There is no fourth floor. A large shopping mall will make up the first five levels of the building. Also, there is no 44th floor. Instead, there will be a level 42A, a level 43 and a level 45."

That made sense to me. After all, I knew there was no 13th floor in most high rises in modern-day, supposedly non-superstitious America.

I was quite impressed with Miss Chen.

"Why do you know so much about Taipei 101?" I asked

"A lot of visitors want to see that building," she explained. "I learn as much as I can about it so I am knowledgeable. My clients like that. They like to see and to learn."

Peter Lee had been right. Julie Chen knew what she was doing.

OCTOBER 1966

While I was in the Army, I tried to live in the moment, especially in Vietnam, where that mindset was highly recommended. Of course, at that point in my life, I didn't have much of a past to reflect upon, and I really didn't seem to care what the future had in store for me. I was nineteen years old and I felt free to do whatever I wanted.

During my first three nights in Taipei, I was like a kid in a candy store. I slept during the day. At night, I prowled the bars in the district just south of the U.S. military's MAAG compound. One after another, I checked out nearly every one of the twenty-six establishments in Taipei authorized to provide female escorts to their customers.

Before you left with a woman, you had to sign a contract. On the first night, I signed out a girl from the Hong Kong Bar. I brought her back to the New China Hotel, located a short cab ride in the south end of the city. We had sex, and that was that.

The next morning, I sent her away. The next night, I signed out a girl from the Susie Wong Bar. The night after that, it was a girl from the OK Bar.

My behavior changed on the fourth night, when I met Mai-Lin in the Little Women Bar, an unpretentious-looking place on a quiet side street around the corner from some of its gaudier competitors. All of the other bars I had visited in Taipei featured plush seating, mirrored walls and indirect lighting designed to show the girls off in the best light, but there was nothing fancy about the Little Women Bar. It had old wooden booths and plain globe lights dangling from its high ceiling.

Unlike the other bargirls I had encountered, Mai-Lin wore a simple blouse and skirt and relatively little makeup. She looked more like an office worker or a college student. Mai-Lin was taller than the other girls I had been with, just a little shorter than I am. Her hair was dark and lustrous.

She had an athletic build with long legs and shapely hips. As I later learned, it was nice to rub up against her.

Perhaps Mai-Lin's best attribute was her radiant smile. It seemed genuine and not plastered on. All of the other bargirls I had met seemed to have a cash register for a heart. Mai-Lin was warm and friendly, a very affectionate person. She also had an infectious laugh, and she got my corny jokes. A plus.

We had good chemistry. We became attached to each other relatively quickly. It didn't matter what we did. We just liked being together, it seemed.

Mai-Lin spoke English reasonably well. Another plus.

The other girls I had been with had spoken little English. At least that was the impression they had given me. I seldom had to ask MaI-Lin to repeat what she said to me. Usually, I was able to decipher her broken English the first time through.

It wasn't spontaneous combustion, but it was close.

As I grew older, I became wary of that phenomenon. After two wives and twice as many live-in girlfriends, I learned that such flash fires burned out just as quickly as they started. I didn't know that then.

I had absolutely no chemistry with the other women I had taken back to the New China Hotel. With all of them, there seemed to be a wall between us. We screwed, but it wasn't that great. Sex is much better between two people who actually like each other. It took me awhile to learn that, too.

April 2002

The heavy traffic slowed us down, and it took nearly a half hour to reach the Imperial.

Parking was at a premium in downtown Taipei, so Miss Chen suggested she tool around the block while I checked in.

Ten minutes later, we headed back to the east side of the city toward Taipei 101. As we drew near, I caught glimpses of the half-completed structure in breaks in the downtown skyline. At more than eight hundred feet, it already eclipsed all the other buildings in Taipei. Because it was erected in a part of the city devoid of skyscrapers, the uncompleted structure looked especially forlorn as we approached it.

We got a lot of work done that afternoon.

First, Miss Chen brought me to a school where a large piece of debris had fallen into a playground. She found an empty space in the school's parking lot. "It's reserved for visitors," she said. "We qualify."

After interviewing the principal and six junior high school students, we walked through the neighborhood.

Next, Miss Chen took me to four noodle stands operating in close proximity to Taipei 101. We talked to some of the customers and to the people who served them. A few times we simply walked up to people on the sidewalk and interviewed them.

At each encounter, Miss Chen broke the ice and then introduced me. I used a small cassette tape recorder. After taping my questions in English, I turned off the device while Miss Chen translated my queries into Mandarin or Taiwanese. Then I turned the recorder back on to tape the answers as she translated the replies into English. It was a cumbersome process, but it worked.

None of the people I interviewed seemed overly concerned about the tower's presence in such a densely-populated part of town. In fact, most of them seemed proud that Taipei would soon be the location of the world's tallest building, more than half a kilometer in height. They didn't seem apprehensive about its toppling over on them.

"They should resume construction as soon as possible," said one man, who intended to seek employment in one of the businesses based in the new skyscraper. "I want to go to work in Taipei 101."

As we slowly strolled through the upscale neighborhood where the skyscraper was being erected, Miss Chen and I looked like two partners in crime.

She carried a huge canvass bag slung over her shoulder, while I toted a dark gray Kensington carrying case containing my laptop, which I seldom let out of my sight when on the road.

Her bag had a picture of a lavender-colored blossom on one side. "What's that," I asked, pointing to the decal.

"A plum blossom," she answered. "A symbol of spring."

I volunteered to add her bag to my load. "It looks heavy."

Miss Chen demurred. "It's all right. It's not as heavy as it looks." Then she added with a laugh: "I carry all my earthly possessions with me. It isn't much."

Her laugh sounded oddly familiar.

OCTOBER 1966

After our first night together, Mai-Lin and I ate breakfast in the small dining room on the first floor of the New China Hotel.

We split a large western omelet and each of us ate a small bowl of corn flakes and drank from a glass of orange juice, which Mai-Lin pronounced "*orangee.*"

"I like," Mai-Lin said, pointing at the bowl of cereal with her spoon. "I think I have for lunch and dinner, too."

We both laughed.

After breakfast, we went for a walk. It was mid-morning, but the streets were deserted. Normally, downtown Taipei was filled with cars, trucks, people on bicycles or in pedicabs and thousands of pedestrians.

"Where is everybody?" I asked.

"Today is Double Ten Day," Mai-Lin said. "Independence Day."

Mai-Lin told me people used to line the streets to watch a large military parade. Technically, the Republic of China was still in a state of war with the mainland Red Chinese. It liked to flex its military muscle.

"No parade today," she said.

"Why not?"

"Two year ago, three jet planes crashed during the parade, so no more parade."

It took her awhile, but Mai-Lin described how one of the jet fighters crashed after clipping a tall radio tower in the north end of the city. The other two jets collided after their pilots were sent to look for the first plane.

After walking for five minutes, we reached the outer periphery of the square in front of the presidential palace. There, tens of thousands of people stood shoulder to shoulder as Chaing Kai-Shek's tinny sing-song voice blasted through loudspeakers.

"What's he saying?" I asked.

She held a finger up to her pursed lips.

We walked in silence for several more minutes, away from the square and from the soldiers who were guarding it.

"Never talk about the generalissimo when other people are near," she explained. "We get into trouble."

We walked for another thirty minutes through the quiet city to the Little Women Bar. It was closed. However, the owner was in his office working on his books. After he responded to our insistent knocks on the front door, I signed Mai-Lin out for another night, my final fling before flying back to Vietnam.

"I know a place where we can go," Mai-Lin said.

We found a cab and headed to the village of Wu Lai in the mountains north of the city. It took about a half hour to reach our destination. On the way, we stopped so Mai-Lin could take a picture with my Instamatic of me standing next to a roadside temple. Then, we had the cabdriver snap a photo of the two of us.

Wu Lai, renowned for its tall waterfall, was supposedly a village made up of Taiwan's aboriginal people. The girls there did dress differently. In contrast to the sexy hip-hugging, high-necked *choengsum* worn by most bar girls, they wore conservative black dresses with red piping and matching tunics. To me, however, in my state of mind, they looked just like every other young female I had encountered in Taiwan.

In order to get to the village, we walked over a narrow suspension bridge and up a large stone stairway to a narrow-gauge set of tracks. While we sat in a small railcar built for two or three people, a man wearing a coolie hat pushed us about a quarter mile down the tracks to the village, which was made up of two or three small thatched huts. A wide stone walkway extended for nearly a hundred meters beyond the huts and was lined with little shops and cafes. The waterfall on the far side of the canyon whooshed hundreds of feet down into the deep gorge.

It was all really unimpressive to a nineteen-year-old boy who definitely had something else on his mind.

We returned to our room at New China Hotel early that evening. We didn't bother to eat dinner.

The next morning I got up at six. Our group from Vietnam was supposed to assemble at the MAAG compound at seven to take the bus to the airport. I showered, shaved, and, for the first time in five days, donned my khaki uniform.

"I really like you," I told Mai-Lin, who remained in bed snugly wrapped in a blanket. "I wish we had met sooner. Now, I have to go back."

"I like you, too," she said. It sounded like she meant it.

"I will come back and see you again."

Mai-Lin shook her head. "No, you can't do that. American soldier in Vietnam have only one R&R. Everyone know that." She held up her index finger for emphasis. "Only one."

"I shall return," I vowed.

Like General McArthur, I intended to keep that promise, but I had no idea how I was going to do it.

April 2002

It was late afternoon by the time Miss Chen drove me back to the Imperial.

She had another gig that evening guiding a group of Australian tourists to some of Taipei's hotter nightspots. I told her I needed some time to transcribe the interviews and file the material in my laptop.

I offered to spring for dinner, but Miss Chen said she would find plenty to nosh on during the pub crawl with the Aussies. She did agree to let me buy her a drink in the hotel's bar.

While I nursed a Sapporo beer and she sipped a Cosmopolitan, I asked Miss Chen how she met Mr. Lee.

"He knew my mother," she said. "They met in Hong Kong not long after I was born."

Miss Chen said Mr. Lee started to correspond with her about the time she started school.

"He would include a little money with the notes he sent to me," she said. "I would ask him about my mother. Where she was? What she was doing? And he always told me he didn't know what happened to her."

Miss Chen explained that she lived in an orphanage run by American Catholic nuns until she was eighteen. It was there that she had learned to speak English, Taiwanese and Chinese Mandarin.

"I suppose I didn't look Chinese enough for westerners to adopt, and I looked too much like a westerner for Chinese to adopt," she explained.

Mr. Lee helped Miss Chen decide on her vocation.

"One time I wrote and asked him what he did for a living," she said. "When he wrote me back describing what he did, I knew I wanted to do the same thing."

Before Miss Chen left, we made a plan to meet again the next morning.

"I have some time during the morning and early afternoon I can devote to you," she said.

"Good," I responded. "By then, I should know exactly how much more material I need."

It was a working dinner. Room service delivered a Caesar salad and a main course of seared codfish with lobster sauce to my suite. As I munched, I listened to the interviews through my headphones.

Miss Chen's voice was easy to listen to. Her English was impeccable, with nary a trace of an accent. Her diction had that homogenous quality so prevalent among those people who do voiceovers for American television commercials. She spoke in a cadence slow enough that I seldom had to rewind the tape.

After three hours of work, I had transcribed all of the interviews and then ran the spell check through one time to clean up my typos. Next, I did some editing. By ten o'clock, my notes were organized. I knew where the story was headed. I felt I had gotten something accomplished.

My room was on the top floor of the twelve-story Imperial. From the large plate-glass windows, I had a good view of downtown Taipei, which was lit up at night. As I looked out over the skyline to the south end of the city, I realized Taipei looked like any other city anywhere in the world.

Somewhere in the direction I was looking stood the New China Hotel, I supposed. It was the first time I had thought about that place since I arrived that morning.

January 1967

Before I left Vietnam for good I managed to wrangle another trip to Taiwan. It took some doing. First, I extended my twelve-month stay in I Corps by another three months to qualify for another five-day leave. Then, I obtained a seat on another R&R flight to Taipei by agreeing to do a favor for a master sergeant in our unit. He pulled some strings.

All I had to do was deliver a small package to a buddy of his stationed with the military advisory group located in the MAAG compound in Taipei. He didn't tell me what was in the small box, enclosed in a plain brown wrapper. I didn't ask.

Night had fallen when the air charter finally arrived at Songshan Airport on my second visit to Taipei. A rocket attack had delayed the departure of the air charter from Da Nang. It had been a long day, and I was beat. I didn't want to go out, so I stayed at the New China Hotel. The concierge found me a girl for the night. She was all right.

The next morning, it was business first. I called the telephone number of the man who was supposed to receive the package. Following his directions, I took a taxi to the U.S. military compound right across the street from where the bus from the airport had dropped us off the night before. As directed, I went to the bowling alley and found an American, who looked to be in his early forties, dressed in civilian clothes sitting at a table in the small snack bar waiting for me.

"There's no need for you to sit," he said. Without a word, I put the package on the table in front of him.

The man looked at it. Then he looked up at me. "Okay," he said. "You've done your job."

I walked out of there and never looked back.

I hailed another cab and headed for the Little Women Bar.

Apparently, I was expected.

"Why you don't come see me last night when you come to Taipei?" Mai-Lin asked.

"What?" I sat in the wooden booth and she towered over me. "How did you know I got in last night?"

"Someone see you when you get off bus from airport."

In a city of one-and-a-half-million people, someone who knew about my connection to Mai-Lin had picked me out of a group of more than a hundred young Americans who had come to Taipei for R&R on my flight. "My god," I joked. "You can tell us apart?"

Mai-Lin didn't laugh. With her arms folded, she looked like a schoolteacher admonishing one of her students for running afoul of the rules.

"Say, what you do last night, anyway?"

I had no choice. I had to fess up. Besides, Mai-Lin probably already knew exactly how I'd spent the evening.

"I was with another girl at the hotel," I admitted. "She's gone now." Then I added sheepishly. "I really didn't like her."

"Hah!" she laughed. "You lie! American boys like all girls."

Then, Mai-Lin, smiling broadly, jumped into the booth next to me, hugged me tightly and kissed me. "It's all right," she purred. "You with Mai-Lin now."

I signed her out for the rest of my stay.

April 2002

I woke up thinking about the first book I had written.

A runaway best seller, "The Favor" had also become the basis of a blockbuster movie. It was a story about a young traveler who is asked by a friend to carry a small package from London to Paris. When the man he is supposed to deliver the package to turns up dead, the young man spends the rest of the book dodging the French police and crooks who want to get their hands on what he's carrying.

It was the story of an unremarkable man thrust into a remarkable situation. That idea became the basis for five more best-selling suspense novels.

Now, I'd hit a roadblock. It seemed I had run out of unremarkable men, remarkable situations or both.

Originally, I thought the trip to Hong Kong might provide me with fodder for another one of those novels. Now, I wasn't so sure. The information I had compiled for the two magazine articles was interesting and the quotes I had collected were telling, but I couldn't see where any of it fit into the writing template I had designed for myself.

Maybe if I spent another day or two in Taipei, a place I was somewhat familiar with, I would trip across something that would get my creative juices flowing again. It had happened before.

JANUARY 1967

Mai-Lin and I didn't spend all our time in bed.

In fact, she was quite adamant about her limits.

"We only do twice a day," she said, holding up two fingers. "If we do two times during the daytime, we don't do at night. OK?"

Anything, it turned out, was okay with me.

No matter what we did, it was fun.

And during our four days together, we did a lot.

Day One included a shopping trip. I bought a Seiko watch for myself, a jade pendant for my mother, and I was measured for a pair of trousers. Mai-Lin probably got a cut of everything I purchased, but I didn't care.

For herself, Mai-Lin, who wore Capri pants and a loose blouse during our shopping trip, purchased a pair of shoes. Flats.

"I tall for a Chinese woman, so I don't wear high heels," she explained. "Men don't like women who are taller than them."

That night, we took in a movie at a large downtown cinema. I must have been the only westerner in the packed audience.

The low-budget black-and-white film *Twenty Four Hours to Kill* was shot on location in Beirut. In it, Mickey Rooney, nearing the end of his movie career, played an airline purser whose greed gets the better of him. During an unscheduled layover in Beirut, his cache of stolen goods brings him to the attention of a smuggler, played by Austrian-born character actor Walter Slezak. Lex Barker, who once played Tarzan, is the pilot who reluctantly tries to bail the avaricious Rooney out.

The movie was subtitled. Chinese and Japanese characters continually changed and burst onto the bottom and left side of the screen. I tried to follow the English dialogue, but I kept trying to decipher those rapidly changing characters as well. It made me dizzy.

Day Two included a trip to the new National Palace Museum, located in a rural area north of the city. Among the exhibits on display were samples of the institution's vast collection of jade objects, including several pieces of carved furniture and a large woven tapestry depicting a Chinese emperor's arrival in Beijing.

That night, Mai-Lin and I took in a floorshow at the 63 Club, a large U.S. military service club located in the city's north end. An orchestra made up entirely of local musicians backed a trio of young American women who were in the midst of a tour of the Orient. It felt like we were at the Copacabana. For that date, Mai-Lin dressed in a short black skirt with a light blue sleeveless blouse and her new shoes.

The next afternoon Mai-Lin and I went on a double date with another girl from the Little Women's Bar and an American Marine. After spending the afternoon at a bowling alley downtown, we had an early dinner at the Mongolian barbecue across the street from the 63 Club.

Mai-Lin and I spent most of Day Four at a bathhouse in Beitou, a small resort town in the mountains north of Taipei famous for its hot springs. During the trip there, our taxi had to stop and wait to make way for two large water buffalo pulling a wagon. The rotten-egg smell of the spa's curative waters killed any desire I had for sex.

That night at the New China Hotel's dining room, Mai-Lin ate filet mignon for the first time. We went to bed early.

APRIL **2002**

Julie Chen arrived at the Imperial Hotel at nine o'clock on the dot.

While we sat in the lobby, I brought her up to speed about what I needed to complete the magazine article.

"We got a lot done yesterday, and I really don't need much more to finish the piece," I told her. "Maybe we could check out other parts of the city and see how the folks there feel about Taipei 101."

Then, I confessed to her. "You know, I have been here before."

"Really?" she seemed surprised. "When?"

I told her about my two visits to Taiwan while I was stationed in South Vietnam.

"I wouldn't mind checking out some of my old haunts," I said.

Miss Chen nodded. "I have no problem with that. Mr. Lee told me always to follow the client's agenda." Another hardy laugh, and she added: "Whatever that means."

We started off slowly by cruising through the narrow city streets near the presidential office complex looking for the New China Hotel.

"I've never heard of that establishment," Miss Chen admitted. "Since Taiwanization, a lot of businesses have changed their names."

"Taiwanization?" I was puzzled.

"About a decade ago, the native Taiwanese, who have always been in the majority here, won control of the government in an election and began a program promoting the island's cultural heritage," she said. "Names of businesses with any connection to China gradually were changed."

"You're part Chinese, right?" I said. "How do you feel about that?"

Miss Chen shrugged. "I don't mind," she said. "The Taiwanese seem to be more accepting of people like me."

"People like you? What do you mean 'people like you'?"

"I am of mixed race," Miss Chen pointed out. "As far as the Chinese are concerned, I am on the bottom rung of the social ladder. At least the Taiwanese allow me to climb it."

JANUARY 1967

During the early part of the last full day of my R&R, Mai-Lin took me to the room where she lived, in a large squat building just down the road from the MAAG compound.

Her living quarters were not much larger than a closet, really.

She shared the small space with another girl from the Little Women Bar. Two sleeping pallets, stacked bunk-bed style, took up one side of the narrow room. At the far end, a metal rod extended across its width. Dresses, skirts, blouses and slacks belonging to both women hung from it. A small bureau sat next to the bed against the wall nearest the door. A single light bulb dangled from the low ceiling.

As I surveyed the room, I noticed a snapshot of a man, another young westerner, sitting on top of the bureau. I picked it up.

"Who's this?" I asked.

"Oh, he Charlie," Mai-Lin volunteered as she stood next to me looking at his picture. "He is Marine from Okinawa. He come visit me three, four times."

"Your boyfriend?"

"I don't know," she shrugged. "Maybe he come see me again, maybe not." No matter what her young Marine did or didn't do, Mai-Lin seemed resigned to it.

As Mai-Lin turned to rummage through the clothes at the other end of the room, I thought about whether I would make another trip to Taipei. I still had five months to go in Vietnam. If I extended for another year, I could get thirty days leave, and I could spend it in Taiwan. I bet my mother would like that.

Up to now, I had been lucky. Our compound inside the old imperial city of Hue had been mortared twice. Also, we took some small arms fire once while I was pulling convoy duty traveling down Route 1 to Da Nang for supplies. Sometimes, my job took me to small Army outposts up in Quang Tri City and down Route 9 toward the Laotian border to Khe Sanh. Those short trips in a deuce-and-half truck were potentially dangerous.

So far, I hadn't so much as nicked myself shaving. Not a scratch. If I got through five more months of Nam, I could go home. I would have to give another extension some more thought.

"I don't know when I will be coming back to see you again," I said abruptly.

Mai-Lin momentarily stopped pawing through the clothes rack, turned and nodded. "I know." She smiled. "Mai-Lin happy now."

When she turned to resume her search, she muttered something in her native tongue.

Maybe I had upset her. "Are you okay?" I asked.

Mai-Lin ran her hands through the line of clothing one more time.

"No find my favorite dress," she said. "I think my friend has it."

Mai-Lin paused to contemplate her next move. "You go back to hotel," she suggested. "I go see her."

"Where is your friend?" I asked.

"She some place," Mai-Lin replied. "I find. You go now."

I was halfway out the door before I stopped to ask her one more question.

"What about tonight?"

Mai-Lin smiled.

"You come to Navy Club at seven o'clock," she said. "I see you there."

April 2002

After our fruitless search for the New China Hotel, I asked Miss Chen to take me to a place I was sure still existed, the waterfall at Wu Lai.

In order to reach that destination, we had to travel across town to the northern suburbs.

As we started the climb into the mountains, I could see how much the landscape had changed since my previous visit nearly thirty-five years before. There was still a lot of greenery, but the city had expanded far beyond its old boundaries. There were large pockets of development all the way along the route.

"When I was a soldier visiting from Vietnam, it was much different here," I told Miss Chen. "People are everywhere now."

Taipei's population had grown by nearly a million during the preceding three decades, Miss Chen said. More than eight million people now lived in the city's metropolitan area.

The waterfall was still there, but Wu Lai had changed. The city had rolled up to the edge of the gorge. The canyon itself was untouched, but I could see rooftops poking up through the trees on the far rim.

Instead of being physically pushed up the tracks to the village by a man wearing a coolie hat, we rode in our own car in a little train that made a tinny sound as it zoomed up the side of the gorge.

The wide stone walkway from which the waterfall on the far side of gorge could be viewed was still there, but it looked like each of the little shops along it had sprouted a second, a third or even a fourth floor.

As we stood gazing at the falls, an elderly man said something to Miss Chen as he strolled past us.

She answered him in one of the Chinese dialects. I could tell from her tone she was not happy with him.

"What did he say?" I asked.

"He told me to have fun with my rich American," she answered.

"What did you tell him?"

"I told him to act his age," Miss Chen said. "Mind his own business."

I looked in the direction of the old man. "Does that happen often?" I asked.

"Occasionally," she smiled. "For me, comments like that are an occupational hazard."

Miss Chen gazed in the direction of the old man, who was slowly walking away from us.

"It's is always someone from his generation," she said. "They think a woman should walk ten feet behind a man when out in public. They live in the past."

I tried to empathize with her. "A lot of people in my country live in the past, too, or at the very least they want to go back there."

Miss Chen became serious.

"I have no past," she said. "I have now and perhaps I have the future. I have no past."

I tried to lighten the mood.

"Well, *this* rich American doesn't mind being taken advantage of." I pointed at a noodle stand. "Are you hungry? Can I spring for lunch?"

January 1967

For my last night in Taipei, Mai-Lin wore a *Cheongsam* for the first time. At seven o'clock, I walked into the Navy Club, located just south of the MAAG compound, to find her sitting with her friend and the young Marine who had gone bowling with us the day before at a table in a mirrored alcove just above the small, sunken dance floor.

Mai-Lin looked radiant. The turquoise form-fitting dress, with its high Manchu collar and slit up one side, enhanced the curve of her hips and the swell of her small breasts. I couldn't take my eyes off her.

For our last date, I wore my new slacks. The dark black pants fit snug around the waist the way I like them, but they were a little baggy in the seat. It didn't matter.

"You look great," I told Mai-Lin.

She beamed.

The acoustics in the small service club were fantastic, and when the first notes of Junior Walker and the All-Stars' *Shotgun* blasted through the sound system, I jumped up to dance with Mai-Lin for the first time.

For a frenzied four minutes, we both bopped, smiling at each other the entire time as we tried to do The Jerk to Walker's raunchy tenor sax. Then, holding each other close on the crowded dance floor, we swayed to the Righteous Brothers' *Unchained Melody*.

In that moment, I thought everything was right with the world. Then, when I sat down after two more fast dances, it hit me. This was going to end. The very next morning, I was going to have to get up, dress in my khakis and head back to South Vietnam. It was cause for contemplation.

While I was lost in thought, apparently staring off into space, the young Marine chatted with Mai-Lin and her friend. Finally, he turned his attention to me. "How come you got that stupid look on your face?" he drawled.

I didn't catch the full import of his question.

"I'm thinking," I said.

The Marine laughed. So did both girls. Everybody got the joke but me.

I never knew the young Marine's real name.

When we had first introduced ourselves to each other at the bowling alley, he drawled: "You can call me Ken. Ken Tucky."

So Ken it was.

As the afternoon went on, he told me about his Vietnam experience. He was a point man for a reconnaissance unit operating in northernmost Quang Tri province.

"Mostly, we're up against regular NVA units," he explained, as we sat watching one of the girls bowl. "Tough boys, who really know what they're doing."

Ken talked about taking arduous day-long hikes through the foothills near the DMZ. "It's all up and down out there," he said. "And you've got to watch every step you take. I took over for a guy who blew off his leg when he stepped on a mine."

Ken told me about how his unit would set up nighttime ambushes. "We'd set up in a crescent maybe twenty yards long," he said. "It was like a little bag with interlocking fields of fire. If Charlie stepped into the bag, he'd get it from two or three different directions at once."

A few times, his squad retrieved the bodies of Marines killed in firefights with the NVA. "Nobody likes to do that job, but we had to go get those guys."

Normally, Army and Marines don't mix, but Ken seemed relieved to be able to share the details about his life in Vietnam. "Don't get me wrong," he said. "I love the Corps, but it's good to get away from all the Semper Fi shit for a while."

APRIL **2002**

Miss Chen ordered a bowl of beef noodle soup for each of us.

"I hope you like tomatoes," she said. "It is a very popular variety, but it is not as spicy as the soup I ordered for myself."

I had always had the knack for getting people to talk about themselves. Maybe, they found me to be a sympathetic person, or at the very least empathetic. With little prodding, it seemed, people would just open and tell me about themselves. In my newspaper days, that ability was definitely helpful. When I began to write novels, some of those people, or at least what they told me, ended up in my books.

It was no different with Miss Chen. I asked just one question, and it sparked a brief but heavy conversation.

"What did you mean when you said 'I have no past?'"

"Exactly that," she answered. Miss Chen used her chopsticks to lift a small piece of braised beef from her bowl. After slowly chewing it, she continued. "I tried to find my mother once, and I was unsuccessful."

Miss Chen told me she went looking for her mother after she left the orphanage. In modern-day Taiwan, the government maintains a registry, and from it children of adoptive parents can find their birth parents, but Miss Chen said the government was unable to help her in her search. There was no record of her birth.

"My mother worked as a bar girl," Miss Chen said. "You know what that is?"

I nodded.

"I tried to find the place where she had worked but it no longer existed, so I gave up looking," she said. "No leads."

"Well, at least you tried," I said.

Miss Chen smiled.

"It's too bad you couldn't find her," I lamented.

She stopped smiling. "That's what I think."

JANUARY 1967

My departure from Taipei was devoid of histrionics.

No tears. No emotional outbursts. No long farewells.

I was going back to Vietnam, and that was that.

I got up at five o'clock, shaved and took a quick shower.

As Mai-Lin lay sleeping, I quietly got dressed and packed my small suitcase. I traveled light.

I left a wad of New Taiwan dollars on the nightstand next to her side of the bed, plus the twenty-dollar bill I kept tucked into a corner of my wallet for emergencies.

Just before I left, I nudged Mai-Lin awake. I leaned over and kissed her forehead.

"Goodbye," I said. "Take care of yourself."

She smiled in reply. Then, she rolled over, wrapped the blankets tightly around her and fell back to sleep.

As I rode in the taxi across town to the MAAG compound, I thought about how easy it had been for me to flip the switch.

Overnight, it seemed, I had gone from being a happy-go-lucky teenager with nary a care in the world back to a grim-faced, serious-minded soldier determined to survive the next five months in Nam.

I was one of the first to arrive at the collection point. Soldiers, sailors and Marines slowly trickled in one by one or in pairs. Conversation was muted. Mostly, we just watched and waited for the bus to take us to the airport.

Apparently, we were all in the same frame of mind. Watching and waiting.

A Marine sergeant was one of the last of our group to show up. When the taxi pulled up, we saw him sitting in the back seat with one arm wrapped around a little bargirl and the other arm wrapped around a giant-sized bottle of Fleishmann's. We continued to watch as he got out of the cab carrying the biggest bottle of vodka we'd ever seen. As he stood behind the car trying to pull his luggage out from the trunk, it appeared that he began haggling with the cabbie over the fare. Before reaching down to grab a suitcase with each hand, the Marine handed the bottle of booze to the girl. Carrying a bottle that was nearly as large as she was, the girl quickly climbed into the back seat. As soon as the Marine handed him the correct sum for the ride, the cabbie, who had been edging back along the driver's side of the car, got into the cab and sped off.

The Marine was left standing there with his two suitcases sitting on the ground beside him. No cab. No girl. No vodka.

"Sonofabitch!" he complained.

The rest of us laughed.

"Slick," I heard someone say admiringly.

"So long, Taiwan," came another voice.

It was just what we needed.

R&R was over. We were ready to go back to the war.

April 2002

Miss Chen and I ate a leisurely lunch. I used a spoon to eat my soup, while Miss Chen only resorted to hers after expertly removing the larger chunks of meat and vegetables from her bowl with her chopsticks.

I asked another question. "When you began your search for your mother how did you know where to look?"

After rummaging through her large canvas bag, which sat in the chair next to her, Miss Chen removed three legal-sized papers that she had placed inside separate acetate sleeves. She slid them across the table to me. Each document was a completed contract for female escort services.

"My mother left these papers at the orphanage when she left me there," she explained. "She told the nuns at the orphanage that one of the men was my father."

All the blanks had been filled in, the dates, the girl's name, the dollar amount and the signature of the man contracting for her company.

I recalled the process. Nearly thirty-five years before, I filled out such paperwork in Taipei. Two of the contracts were dated just a day apart in October, 1966, and the third was dated the following January and covered a four-day period.

When I looked at the signatures, I received a jolt. One contract was signed by A. Lincoln. G.A. Custer had signed another one. Millard Fillmore's name was at the bottom of the third contract. It was my handwriting.

I quickly regained my composure. "You know who these men are, don't you?"

Miss Chen nodded. "I know they were two American presidents and a famous American general. I was told my father was one of these men."

I again looked at the three dates.

"When were you born, Miss Chen?"

"I was born in July 1967," she answered. "That was why I was named Julie."

After quickly doing the math, I realized Mai-Lin already was pregnant when I visited Taipei the second time. She must have known she was carrying a baby. Why didn't she tell me about her condition? She must have suspected I was the father but kept it a secret.

"So you really don't know who your father was?"

Miss Chen shook her head. "Not a clue."

I thought for a moment. Then I pushed the bowl of soup away from me.

"Let's take a walk," I said. "I want to tell you a story."

Before we stepped onto the strand for our stroll, I reached into a pocket inside my computer bag for the faded snapshot of Mai-Lin and me standing together.

OLD
FLAME

SEPTEMBER 2014

If she hadn't had said "hello," I never would have recognized her. There we were, sitting next to each other in a waiting room in a hospital in Norway, Maine, and I had no clue that the elderly woman sitting next to me was the auburn-haired, fair-skinned, blue-eyed girl I had been engaged to marry nearly fifty years before.

"Don't you remember me?" she asked, after addressing me by name.

"How, how do you know my name?" I was quite perplexed.

"I heard the nurse say it," she explained.

The nurse had guided me to the waiting room after a medical technician left us to wheel the gurney carrying my wife down the hall for x-rays. She had tripped while walking down the path to Snow Falls, a picturesque waterfall off Route 26 between Bethel and South Paris. My wife claimed she wasn't in much pain, but we decided to stop at the hospital to have her checked out.

"I'm sorry," I began. "I am usually pretty good with faces, but I just can't place you."

Then she said her name.

Instantly, the memories flooded in.

Ours had been a whirlwind romance, lasting only a matter of weeks, or, more accurately, a matter of weekends. We fell madly in love during the first two months of 1966, toward the end of my stay at the United States Army Security Agency Training Center at Fort Devens in Massachusetts. I'd joined the Army the summer before, a month after graduating from high school. When the romance began, I was winding up a sixteen-week course in traffic analysis before shipping out to South Vietnam. The Army was teaching me how to be a spook.

She and I had met during my senior year. She was going out with someone else at the time, but she seemed really friendly and was in the final throes of that relationship when we saw each other again after I got out of basic training the following fall. When we met for the third time, during the weekend after New Year's, sparks flew.

While wrapping up the ASA training course, I hitchhiked every weekend back to Augusta. We spent nearly every minute we had together in the apartment she shared with a friend from high school. For a couple of teenagers, it was paradise. We couldn't keep our hands off of each other. We vowed it would always be like that.

During one of my final weekends home, we took a walk downtown. We stopped and window-shopped at the little jewelry store that used to be on the corner of Water and Bridge Streets. From the look in her eyes, I could tell she wanted a ring, so we went inside and she picked one out. It seemed like a good idea at the time. The storeowner happened to be a cousin of mine, another member of our large French-Canadian clan. He let me buy the ring on time. It took two of my tax-free Vietnam paychecks to pay it off.

The last time I saw my fiancee I was boarding a plane at Logan for the trip west to the Army replacement depot in Oakland. She had accompanied my parents on the drive to Boston to see me off. That was in late February.

"You haven't changed much," she said to me now.

She lied. I had gained more than sixty pounds and my dark curly hair had been replaced with a bald pate surrounded by lots of gray hair on its fringes.

"You look good." I lied, too. Her wavy auburn hair was gone, replaced by short straight tresses of pure gray. Her milky-white skin was lined and weathered, and her blue eyes, which used to light up at the sight of me, had a steely cast to them.

"I was very angry with you," she said.

She had earned the right. I probably was one of the few guys who broke off an engagement while stationed in South Vietnam. At the time I wrote the "Dear Joan" letter, I was nineteen. I had joined the ASA, one of the three military affiliates of the ultra-secret National Security Agency, right out of high school. It was a four-year hitch, and I still had three years to go when I wrote my final letter to her. In it, I told her I didn't want to get married. I didn't know what the Army had in store for me, I said, and I didn't want her to wait for something that might not happen.

"I thought you really played me," she said.

"If I did, I was totally unaware of it," I responded. "I really cared for you, and I wanted you to be happy."

As it turned out, I spent nearly another year in Nam after I wrote the letter. By the time I got back home, she had gotten married and was about to become a mother for the first time.

My thoughts returned to the present.

"What are you doing here?" I asked. "You're all right, aren't you?"

During our entire conversation, her expression remained the same. She didn't appear happy to see me nor upset to find me sitting next to her after an absence of nearly fifty years. She just looked grim. It was an expression that seemed permanent.

"I'm looking after a friend," she said.

"Nothing serious, I hope?"

She shook her head. "No, nothing serious."

"What about you?" she asked. "What are you doing here?"

"It's my wife," I said. "She fell during a walk in the woods and they're just checking to make sure she didn't break anything."

"Oh," she said. "The wife."

It was awkward. It was clear she really didn't want to talk about what the past five decades had been like for her. And I really didn't want to volunteer any information either. Why open old wounds?

I could have told her about how my wife and I met. About the forty years we'd spent together. About our two sons. Our grandson. My career.

But none of that seemed relevant or pertinent to the slim connection we now had.

From her haggard, world-weary appearance, I deduced she had had a rough time of it. Her life apparently had been difficult, and she wasn't going to share the details. I wasn't going to pry.

Presently, a nurse called out my name.

"You wife is back from x-ray," she announced. "You can see her now."

Before I stood up, I reached over and touched my former fiancee's hand. I gave it a little squeeze. To my relief, she didn't recoil.

"It was nice seeing you again," I said. "I really mean that."

When she replied, there was a hint of a smile. "Ditto," she said.

As I hurried down the hall toward the ER, I thought about what I was going to say to my wife. She knew all about the engagement and the letter I wrote from Vietnam ending it, but she had never met the woman.

When I got back to my wife's room, I found her sitting in a wheel-chair and a young doctor was standing next to her.

"The x-rays were negative," the doctor announced. "Nothing's broken, but there is a little swelling. Apply some ice and pop a couple of Tylenol and you should be good to go."

I looked down at my wife. "How do you feel, hon?"

"All right," she said. "I just want to go home."

Before he signed off, the doctor told my wife that she should use crutches for two or three days. "You can walk with the crutches," he explained. "Just don't put your full weight on that leg for a couple of days."

Crutches? It was the weekend. Where were we going to get crutches? As usual, my wife had the answer. That was one of the reasons I loved her.

"Before we go to the house, we can go to town to Hannaford," she explained as I walked next to her, the nurse slowly wheeling her down the hall from the ER. "We can get them for free from the store pharmacy. We pay a twenty-dollar deposit, and we get the money back when we return the crutches."

I looked at my watch. We still had an hour's drive ahead of us. If we booked it, we could make it to Hannaford before the pharmacy closed. It was a good plan.

As we neared the waiting room, my stomach began to churn. I hadn't settled on just what I was going to do when we got there. Should I make formal introductions? Should I simply nod to my former fiancee as we rolled past? Or should I just point her out to my wife as we left the room? The permutations ran through my mind.

As our entourage entered the waiting room, I was shocked. She was gone It was as if she had never been there at all. I was totally relieved.

My wife must have picked up my vibe.

"Are you all right?" she asked.

"I'm just fine." I answered. "Just fine."

THE CONSTITUTIONAL

JANUARY 2015

Every Wednesday, my wife and I took a walk along the bike path next to the river in Brunswick. Actually, I walked. She jogged. Between us, we had one good set of knees. Unfortunately, the two healthy joints weren't part of the same body.

During two arthroscopic surgeries, the meniscus in my wife's right knee had been clipped to a nub. She was constantly complaining of a twitching feeling. "The knee's going to lock up again," she'd say. "I know it. I can feel it." Yet, she refused to have an orthopedic surgeon take another stab at repairing the damage. "I'm all done having someone tinker with my knee."

Five years before, while celebrating my sixth-fifth birthday, I fell off the deck on the back of my house and tore the quadriceps muscle just above my left knee. (I was sober as a judge, honest.) My foot got caught in one of the risers on the stairs. I ripped the muscle completely as I fell to the ground. I heard it pop. The surgeon repaired the quad by drilling three holes through my kneecap, uncoiling the separated parts of the muscle and threading the ends through the holes.

Despite months and months of rehab, the knee has never been the same. There's always pain, or at the very least discomfort somewhere in that joint. It's like that giant stormy spot on the planet Jupiter. One day, the tightness is in one place. The next day, it's somewhere else.

On most days, other than Wednesdays, my wife and I took our dog and started our walk by meandering through the network of streets in our development of small ranches and capes off Jordan Avenue.

I would lead Skippy, a short-legged black Lab/Beagle mix, on a leash while my wife jogged the mile-long circuit. I walked at the dog's pace. Skippy stopped every once in a while to sniff a clutch of bushes or a utility pole before squatting to leave her own mark. Sometimes, my wife would cover the course twice before Skippy and I finished our walk.

But on Wednesdays, my wife insisted we take a jaunt without the dog along the two-and-a-half mile stretch of paved walkway that runs alongside the Androscoggin River from Water Street to Cooks Corner, Brunswick's shopping mecca.

"Come on, Sweet Potato, get off the couch," she'd announce. "It's time for our constitutional."

We were just like the postal service. Wind, rain, sleet or snow. It didn't matter. We were taking that walk. Like I said, I walked. She jogged. She went ahead, and I gamely tried to keep up. I never made it to the end of the trail before meeting up with my wife on her return trip from Brunswick's east end.

On one such Wednesday, after a brief thaw, the bitterly cold Maine winter had settled back in. The night before, a light snow had deposited an inch or so of powder on the ground. The steady wind whipping down the river now enveloped the bike path in a fine mist composed of the white stuff.

As usual, my wife stepped out ahead of me. Within moments, she was out of sight, lost in the wind-blown snow.

I kept walking at my own pace. After about fifteen minutes, I stopped to take a break on a large stone bench overlooking a wide stretch of the Androscoggin about three quarters of a mile down the bike path.

I wasn't out of breath, but my knee was killing me. Sometimes when I walked, especially on frigid winter days, it felt like the joint was caught in the grip of a giant vice. The more I walked the tighter its hold became. Usually, when I stopped walking for a few minutes, it would loosen up.

Also, my nose was running, and, when I reached into my pocket to fish out a hanky, I discovered I hadn't brought one with me. Instead, I used the sleeve of my ski parka to wipe my nose. It didn't help.

With my knee hurting and snot running down close to my upper lip, I sat staring out at the cloud of wind-whipped snow that seemed to hover over the frozen river.

Normally, after a brief respite, I'd get back on the cleared walkway and head in the direction my wife took. But instead of following her, I started walking back to our Volvo, which sat alone in the parking lot at the head of the trail.

Ten minutes later, my wife caught up with me. She hadn't completed her run to Cooks Corner. Somewhere along the way, she had turned around and had run back to me. "What's the matter?" she asked, slowing her pace to match mine.

"I just can't do this anymore," I said. I took another useless swipe at my nose with my sleeve. "This is killing me."

"But this is supposed to be good for us," she explained.

When I looked down at my wife, I noted her slight limp. I ignored it. Instead, I complained. "You know, you take better care of the dog than you do me."

It was true. When Skippy exhibited the slightest limp in her walk, my wife would be off to the vet with her. Glucosamine would be prescribed and the dog seemed to rebound after a few doses.

An upset stomach prompted another quick trip to the veterinary clinic. "When she's outside, don't let her eat something she shouldn't," the vet reminded my wife. "I'll tell my husband," she'd responded. "That's his department."

Because of the wind, we huddled closer together as we walked. I am heavyset and stand nearly a head taller than my wife, so I tried to use my bulk to shield her from the cold biting wind coming off the river as we headed toward the parking lot.

"Look," I said. "I want to grow old with you, but I don't want to be run into the ground doing it."

"I just want us to be healthy," she countered. "I thought running, I mean, walking would be good for us."

As we moved along, my knee began to tighten up again. "The walks are all right, I guess, but it always turns into a race, and I just can't keep up. I don't want to spend the rest of my life chasing after you."

"You use to like to chase me," she joked.

"I know," I smiled. "Now you've got to make it easier for me to catch you, I guess."

We walked on for a few minutes without talking; each lost in our own thoughts. As we strolled beneath the bridge spanning the river, I could hear the hum of the cars traveling between Brunswick and Topsham.

When our Volvo came into view, my wife broke the silence.

"We'll go home now," she said. "I'll make some hot chocolate. Tomorrow, we'll take a walk around the neighborhood with Skippy."

Then, after linking an arms and taking a few more steps, she added: "Weather permitting."

ACKNOWLEDGEMENTS

Writing a book is always a journey, and I had plenty of company on this trip.

As usual, I got a big assist from my wife, Debbie. She lets me know when I'm headed in the wrong direction, which is more often than I'd like to admit.

Early on, Lisa Wesel, a former newspaper colleague, encouraged me to work in the short-story form. Her recommendations on a lot of these stories were spot-on.

I owe a big thanks to Molly McGrath, a top-notch copy editor who cleaned up my messes and helped make the narrative crisper and more precise.

In addition to providing me with a pat on the back, first-readers Andy Cusack, Sally Foster, Steve Solloway and Edda Briggs Thiel delivered important feedback. These folks come from a wide variety of backgrounds. Among them are the owner of a motor speedway, a retired English teacher, an award-winning sports columnist and the former proprietor of a bookshop. All of them have one thing in common — a love of books.

Thanks also go to Bruce Redwine, a fellow Vietnam War vet who brought me up to date on certain aspects of Chinese culture, and to Jim Bleikamp, a broadcast veteran who helped refresh the memories of my own radio days.

FOLLOW THE EXCITING ADVENTURES OF CID INVESTIGATOR JOHN MURPHY

Phu Bai: In 1967, the United States military involvement in South Vietnam is reaching its zenith. As the war rachets up, John Murphy and Charles Van Dyck of the Army's Criminal Investigation Division investigate the murder of an American soldier at Phu Bai. War intrudes as the two investigators build their case against the most likely suspect. But a bizarre twist leads to an unusual manhunt in the middle of a war zone.

Kagnew Station: In 1968, Army CID investigator John Murphy travels to a remote U.S. military base in Ethiopia to find the murderer of an American soldier. Evidence points to a marauding band of Eritrean rebels. The investigation becomes personal when someone to tries to kill Murphy, still coming to grips with his Vietnam War experience. Murphy uncovers the identity of the killer but faces an unusual dilemma while wrapping up the case.

The Man In The Canal: In 1971, Army CID investigator John Murphy goes undercover to find a murderer hiding among the U.S. military deserters taken refuge in Sweden during the Vietnam War. Simultaneously, Swedish police inspector Magnus Lund tries to learn the identity of a dead man found floating the historic Gota Canal. The two investigators work separately until the thread of clues bring them together for an exciting climax.

Mr. Betit's books are available in soft-cover and e-book editions on Amazon.com <http://amazon.com/>

www.ingramcontent.com/pod-product-compliance
Lightning Source LLC
Chambersburg PA
CBHW071005120726
47910CB00004B/1396